Through The Eyes of Longinus

John H Brennan

Published by John H Brennan, 2024.

This is a work of fiction. Similarities to real people, places, or events are entirely coincidental.

THROUGH THE EYES OF LONGINUS

First edition. March 5, 2024.

Copyright © 2024 John H Brennan.

ISBN: 979-8224113170

Written by John H Brennan.

To those of you who pray and are inspired by the Holy Spirit,
that you take your vocation to be Christ's Disciple seriously,
starting today!

Introduction

There is a tradition and some later apocryphal writings that attempt to name the centurion at the crucifixion of Jesus. However, the names, "Longinus" and "Cassius" seem to rise to the top of most lists. But neither are not found in the canonical Gospels of the Bible, and their use comes from later sources and traditions.

The Gospel accounts, Matthew, Mark, Luke and John, do not provide a specific name for the centurion who declared Jesus to be the Son of God at Golgotha. The emphasis in the biblical narrative is on the statement itself and the recognition of Jesus' divine nature rather than on the identity of the individual making the declaration. The names mentioned in later traditions are not considered part of the authoritative biblical account.

I liked the name Longinus the best, so throughout this book, I will use that name. Because there is so little factual information documented anywhere about this centurion as well as the fact that I tend to ask the Holy Spirit myself to plant in my mind the seeds that would sprout into the words of this book. And by the way, my apologies to those who prefer Cassius! So who was this man, Longinus and what was his mission?

In the shadows of intrigue and political maneuvering, Longinus operated as an independent intelligence agent for the Roman Army, his role transcending the conventional duties implied by his title of centurion. Tasked directly by Caesar, his mission carried the weight of assessing a burgeoning conflict in Jerusalem, one fueled by the rising influence of a Jewish Rabbi named Jesus.

Rumors had traversed the vast expanse from Jerusalem to Rome, whispers of an impending clash between the Jewish leaders entrenched in the sacred halls of the temple and the fervent followers of this enigmatic Rabbi. In a remarkably short span of three years, Jesus had ascended to a stature of popularity that raised eyebrows even within the vast bureaucracy of the Roman Empire.

Jesus, a preacher whose words resonated with an unwavering conviction, wielded a charisma that reached beyond the ordinary. His teachings, marked by an unconventional blend of wisdom and spirituality, had captured the hearts of many. Yet, it was the tales of miracles—feats that defied the laws of nature—that elevated him to a status akin to that of a superstar in the eyes of his followers.

This phenomenon was not lost on Longinus, who approached his mission with a discerning eye. The purported miracles, whether the turning of water into wine, the healing of the sick, or the walking on water, left a trail of awe and wonder in their wake. The allure of such extraordinary acts drew crowds from Judea and the surrounding regions, creating a movement that posed a palpable threat to the established order.

Longinus delved into the heart of this burgeoning conflict, seeking to understand the dynamics that fueled the tension between Jesus and the Jewish leaders. His assessment went beyond the superficial, probing the motivations of both sides and examining the potential implications for Roman interests in the region.

The threat posed by a charismatic figure who could rally the masses with a blend of captivating rhetoric and inexplicable wonders was not to be underestimated. Longinus, with a keen intellect honed by years of military service and covert operations, navigated the complex landscape of religious fervor and political intrigue.

His role as an independent agent allowed him to operate in the shadows, observing the unfolding drama without the constraints of overt military authority. Longinus assessed the loyalty of Jesus' followers, delving into the psychology of devotion that bound them to their Rabbi. The intensity of this loyalty, coupled with the potential for a clash with the established order, became a focal point in Longinus' reports to Caesar.

As the clash between Jesus and the Jewish leaders loomed on the horizon, Longinus understood that the outcome of this conflict could reverberate far beyond the streets of Jerusalem. The fragile balance of power, both religious and political, teetered on the edge, and Longinus, the astute intelligence agent, stood at the nexus of a storm that had the potential to reshape the very foundations of the Roman Empire's presence in the tumultuous lands of Judea.

Here is a teaser of what is ahead...

In the dim twilight of ancient Jerusalem, the seasoned centurion Longinus gazed upon the unfolding events at Golgotha. His weathered armor bore witness to countless battles, but nothing had prepared him for the extraordinary scene that was playing out before his eyes.

As the earth trembled beneath his feet and the skies darkened, Longinus couldn't help but feel a shiver run down his spine. He had commanded cohorts and stood unfazed in the face of adversaries, but this crucifixion was different. The air was heavy with an otherworldly intensity.

Longinus, a man of duty and discipline, had seen many criminals meet their fate on the cross. Yet, the man hanging there, bloodied and crowned with thorns, radiated a presence that defied explanation. Whispers of his deeds and miracles had reached the ears of this Roman centurion, and now, in this moment, Longinus found himself questioning the very nature of the world he thought he knew.

His fellow soldiers, hardened by years of service, exchanged uneasy glances as the ground quivered beneath them. In that moment, Longinus felt a stirring within his soul. A conviction that this man, condemned to die, was no ordinary criminal.

As the sun dipped below the horizon, Longinus stood transfixed, unable to tear his gaze away from the scene. The words escaped his lips almost involuntarily, "Truly, this was the Son of God."

In the aftermath of that fateful day, Longinus found himself haunted by the memory of the crucifixion. The declaration he had made echoed in his mind, challenging the very core of his beliefs. A man of duty had become a witness to the divine, forever.

I am Longinus

"I am Longinus, a Centurion in the Roman Army, bearing the weight of countless campaigns and battles. I report to the esteemed commanders of the legions, a servant of Rome's unyielding might. My years of service have been etched into the very fabric of my armor, each scar telling a tale of victories and challenges faced in the name of the empire.

I have commanded cohorts on the fringes of the known world, from the arid deserts to the mist-covered forests. The clash of steel, the roar of the legions, and the disciplined march of my men are the rhythms of my existence. I am a guardian of the Roman way, a centurion forged in the crucible of discipline and duty.

My leadership has been tested in the chaos of battle, where the line between life and death is as thin as the blade of my gladius. I have stood unyielding against the onslaught of foes, rallying my men with the might of Rome coursing through our veins. Victory is not just a goal; it is the very essence of our being.

To attain the esteemed rank of Centurion in the Roman Army is no simple feat. It demands more than skill with a sword or mastery of battlefield tactics; it requires a steadfast commitment to the principles that define the might of Rome.

To become a Centurion, one must first prove their mettle as a soldier in the lower ranks. I, Longinus, began my journey as a mere legionary, marching in formation and honing my skills under the watchful eye of seasoned centurions. Discipline, loyalty, and unwavering dedication to the empire's cause form the bedrock of a centurion's character.

Aspiring Centurions must navigate the ranks, showcasing leadership in the heat of battle and displaying an unyielding adherence to the chain of command. Merely surviving the rigors of the Roman military is not enough; one must thrive in adversity and emerge as a natural leader among their peers.

Upon achieving the rank of Optio, a subordinate officer, the true crucible begins. It is here that leadership skills are scrutinized, tactical acumen is tested, and the ability to inspire and command is brought to the forefront. Only those who distinguish themselves with valor and competence ascend to the prestigious role of Centurion.

A Centurion is more than a warrior; they are the embodiment of Rome's strength and discipline. They lead from the front, instilling confidence in their men through example and unwavering determination. The loyalty of the soldiers under their command is earned through shared hardships, victories, and the undeniable respect inspired by a true leader.

In the end, it is not just the armor, the gladius, or the plume-adorned helmet that defines a Centurion. It is the indomitable spirit, the unshakable commitment to Rome, and the ability to lead in both triumph and tribulation that sets a Centurion apart—a position I, Longinus, hold with pride and humility."

More about Me and My Mission

I entered the legionary ranks at a youthful age, fueled by a fervent desire to serve the empire and carve my place in the annals of history. In my prime, the call to don the lorica and embrace the life of a soldier resonated deeply within me. The decision to join the legions was not merely a career choice; it was a commitment to a higher calling.

As a young man, the allure of adventure and the promise of glory on the battlefield were magnetic. The Roman Empire offered an avenue for ambition, a chance to rise above the ordinary and leave an indelible mark. To be a part of something greater than oneself, to defend the ideals of Rome and march in the footsteps of legendary commanders—this was the dream that kindled the flames of passion within my heart.

The reasons for a man of my age to join the legions are as varied as the individuals who march alongside me. Some seek escape from the mundane, craving the excitement of foreign lands and the camaraderie forged in the crucible of conflict. Others, like myself, are driven by a sense of duty, a profound allegiance to the grand tapestry that is Rome.

Yet, the path to becoming a Centurion is no fleeting pursuit. It demands a longevity of service, a dedication that withstands the test of time. The years in the legions have not only molded me into a seasoned warrior but have instilled in me the wisdom that comes with enduring the ebb and flow of campaigns.

As I stand now, a Centurion with a career etched in battles and conquests, I look back at that young recruit and recognize the journey from eager legionary to seasoned leader. The vigor of youth has given way to the tempered strength of experience, and through it all, the unwavering commitment to Rome remains the guiding force that defines my existence."

The Roman Empire was known for its vast and diverse territories, and the assignment of centurions to different regions was based on the strategic and administrative needs of the empire. Jerusalem, being a crucial city in the Roman province of Judea, held significant importance due to its historical, cultural, and religious significance.

Centurions were often deployed to maintain order and enforce Roman authority in regions where there was a potential for unrest or resistance. Jerusalem, with its diverse population and the presence of different religious and cultural groups, was prone to periodic tensions. The Romans aimed to ensure stability, prevent rebellions, and secure the loyalty of the local populace.

Additionally, the Roman Empire had a practice of stationing experienced and capable officers in key provinces. Jerusalem, being a focal point for the administration of Judea, required skilled leaders to navigate the complexities of the region. Centurions with a proven track record of leadership and discipline would be chosen to serve in such critical assignments.

In the case of a centurion like me, my posting in Jerusalem was the result of my demonstrated abilities in maintaining order and executing the will of the Roman authorities. My role would involve overseeing the Roman garrison, ensuring compliance with Roman laws, as well as assessing and managing any potential challenges to Roman rule in the region. The deployment of centurions like me to such sensitive areas was a testament to the Roman strategy of maintaining control and stability throughout their vast empire.

About my Assignment

In the vast expanse of the Roman Empire, provinces like Judea were typically under the jurisdiction of a Roman governor rather than directly under the control of the emperor Caesar. Pontius Pilate served as the Roman governor, sometimes referred to as "prefect" of Judea for the last seven years or so.

I was in Jerusalem on a special assignment related to maintaining order and security, especially during a potentially tumultuous period like Passover. I reported to and take orders from the local Roman governor, Pontius Pilate, but he knew that Ceaser handpicked me to come to Jerusalem to assess the situation and direct efforts to maintain order. The governor had authority over military matters, civil administration, and the overall stability of the province. Therefore, I would mostly work undercover on intelligence and advise the governor on areas he should direct resources to.

This had the potential for some very interesting dynamics between Pilate and me, considering the power structure and the delicate balance between Roman authority, local politics, and the potential religious tensions in Judea. But he is the governor, so I will honor that position in how I will move forward on this assignment.

The Trip To My New Assignment

As I received the unexpected orders to leave the heart of Rome and embark on the journey back to Jerusalem, a whirlwind of thoughts and emotions enveloped me. The imperial orders, bearing the weight of unseen concerns and a sense of urgency, felt strangely familiar yet charged with an unparalleled significance.

As the chariot wheels rumbled along the well-trodden roads, I couldn't escape the contrast between the grandeur of Rome and the dust-laden paths toward Judea. Memories of my past service in Jerusalem resurfaced, each turn in the road echoing the challenges and complexities of this ancient city. The crowds, the narrow streets, the religious fervor—Jerusalem held a unique place in my history.

The journey itself became a voyage through the chapters of my life. The landscapes changed, but the anticipation grew. In my possession, the imperial seal bore witness to the unseen currents of power that dictated my return. Caesar's concerns about potential disruptions during Passover lingered in my thoughts, painting the festival as a paradox of peace and potential unrest.

The cuisine of Rome, with its rich flavors and diverse offerings, had been left behind. In their place, the foods of Judea accompanied my journey—a subtle reminder of the region's unique character. The taste of olives, figs, and the aroma of spices permeated the air as I traversed the landscapes, each meal becoming a reflection of the cultural tapestry that awaited me in Jerusalem.

Arriving at the city gates, the echoes of ancient history resonated. The details I brought with me from Rome, meticulously packed and sealed, held the weight of authority. Scrolls, reports, and the imperial directives were my companions, each bearing the signature of Caesar himself. The intricate details of Roman governance, the subtleties of diplomacy, and the lessons learned on the battlefields were all part of the baggage I carried, both physical and metaphorical.

Before meeting Pilate, the governor of Judea, I found myself reflecting on the path that led me back to this city. The journey transcended geographical boundaries, becoming a pilgrimage through the corridors of power, duty, and a destiny intricately woven into the fabric of Roman history. The air was thick with anticipation, and as I stepped onto Jerusalem's soil, I couldn't shake the feeling that this chapter, like the city itself, held the promise of both challenge and revelation.

Meeting With The Governor

The journey was not just geographical; it was a pilgrimage through my own history. The gates of Jerusalem, with their ancient grandeur, loomed ahead. The city, a mosaic of cultures and faiths, held both the echoes of past challenges and the potential for new complexities.

Only once had I met Pilate since he assumed the mantle of governor. The memory of that encounter lingered, etched with the apprehension of the unknown. Pilate, with his reserved demeanor and the weight of Roman authority in his gaze, presented an enigma that unsettled even seasoned centurions like myself.

Arriving uninvited, a detail of Roman soldiers in tow, was a gamble. The governor's response to such an intrusion was unpredictable. The delicacies of diplomacy, an art not unfamiliar to me, needed to be wielded with precision in the face of Pilate's authority. As the chariot neared the heart of Jerusalem, my mind buzzed with the intricacies of the path ahead — a path that intertwined duty, history, and the palpable uncertainty of the present.

As we approached the governor's palace, I couldn't help but feel a subtle tension in the air. The significance of our unannounced arrival, combined with the memories of our previous encounter, added weight to the impending reunion. Pilate must have known I was coming; my orders were not mere whispers in the wind. The decision to arrive uninvited was a calculated move, a statement of the urgency and gravity of the situation.

The imposing gates of the palace loomed ahead, guarded by Roman sentinels whose helmets gleamed in the Judean sun. As we halted before the entrance, I dismounted my horse, the clink of armor accompanying each step toward the entrance.

A servant, recognizing the Roman insignia, ushered me into the vestibule. The air was heavy with a mix of anticipation and formality. Awaiting an audience with Pilate, I couldn't escape the feeling that our encounter would set the tone for the days to come.

The door to Pilate's audience chamber swung open, revealing the austere figure of the governor himself. His gaze, steady and calculating, met mine. The air hung with an unspoken acknowledgment of the complexities that bound our paths.

"Pontius Pilate," I saluted, the gravity of our surroundings amplifying the resonance of my words. "I come at the behest of Caesar, sent to ensure order and security during this Passover season."

Pilate's response was measured, his expression revealing little. The dynamics between us were delicate, the unspoken understanding of Roman hierarchy and duty weaving through the air. Our initial reunion, set against the backdrop of the governor's palace, marked the beginning of a chapter in Jerusalem fraught with political intricacies and the ever-present specter of the unknown.

Pilate simply said "My Tribune will arrange your quarters." With that, he turned and walked further into the palace and the inner doors closed.

As the days unfolded in Jerusalem, Pontius Pilate summoned me to his residence, indicating a need for a detailed exchange of information. The urgency in his request resonated with a tone of gravity, prompting me to gather my thoughts and make my way to the governor's palace.

The sun cast long shadows across the courtyard as I approached the entrance of Pilate's residence. The Roman guards stationed at the gate acknowledged my presence, and with a nod, I was permitted to enter.

The corridors, adorned with ornate Roman decorations, echoed with the weight of power and political machinations.

Upon reaching the inner chambers, I was met by the stern countenance of Pilate's Tribune, a man whose authority matched his reputation. Pilate, seated behind a grand desk, gestured for both of us to be seated as the door closed behind us.

"Longinus, this is my trusted officer, Marcus Quintus. He oversees matters of security in Jerusalem," Pilate stated, acknowledging the officer by his side.

Marcus Quintus and I exchanged a curt nod, the unspoken understanding of the responsibilities that bound us in this volatile city. Pilate wasted no time, diving into the core of our meeting.

Pilate began, "intelligence has reached me regarding a certain individual from Nazareth, Jesus they call him. It seems he has gained a following, stirring the crowds with talk of miracles and divine authority."

Marcus Quintus and I listened intently, the gravity of the situation settling over us. Pilate continued, detailing reports of the increasing tensions between Jesus and the Jewish religious leaders, their concern over his influence during the Passover season, and the potential for civil unrest.

"The religious authorities are pressing for action," Pilate stated, his eyes shifting between us. "They fear that this man's influence could spark a rebellion. We need a thorough understanding of the situation, Longinus. Marcus Quintus will share with you all that we have gathered so far."

Marcus Quintus leaned forward, producing scrolls containing intelligence reports and sketches of key figures. His demeanor was focused, a reflection of the seriousness of the task at hand.

"We have eyes and ears in the city," Marcus Quintus began. "Reports suggest that Jesus has been gathering a diverse following, with whispers of healings and miraculous events. However, the dynamics are complex.

Some see him as a prophet, while others view him as a threat to the established order."

As he spoke, the details unfolded — the gatherings on the Mount of Olives, the sermons in the temple, and the subtle alliances forming among Jesus' followers. The intricate web of loyalties and tensions within Jerusalem became clearer.

Pilate's gaze remained fixed on us, his silence prompting Marcus Quintus to conclude the briefing. "Longinus, we must tread carefully. The religious leaders are influential, and any misstep could tip the delicate balance we maintain in this city. I trust you to assess the situation and ensure that Rome's interests are safeguarded."

The weight of the responsibility settled upon me as I absorbed the gravity of the intelligence shared. Pilate's eyes bore into mine, and Marcus Quintus awaited my response. The delicate dance between political maneuvering, local dynamics, and the mysterious figure of Jesus set the stage for a chapter in Jerusalem that would test not only our fortitude as Romans but the very fabric of power and influence in this ancient city.

The Sanhedrin was the Jewish council in Jerusalem, consisting of priests, elders, and scholars. I knew that Marcus would have input on the various influential members may have had insights into the religious and political climate.

Marcus got into the details about the religious leaders who played significant roles in the Jewish community, so that I would know who to interact with to gather intelligence about Jesus and the potential for unrest during the Passover season. First was the High Priest Caiaphas. Caiaphas has been the high priest for the last fifteen years. He lived in an elaborate home on Mount of Olives, directly across the Kidron Valley from the Temple. His home was large enough to hold secret meetings with the other religious leaders without anyone noticing. We believe that is why he chose to live outside the gates. He also has a cell, to hold people prisoner. We have a good idea what he and his men do to those prisoners.

Next Marcus continued, is Annas. Annas was the father-in-law of Caiaphas and, though not officially serving as high priest, he was influential and played a significant role in the religious politics of the day. He lived with Caiaphas and certainly had his ear.

Although primarily known as a Pharisee and a member of the Sanhedrin, Nicodemus is a very open-minded leader. He appears to provide a balanced perspective from within the religious elite. But there are rumors from a scout revealing interesting activities of Nicodemus. The esteemed Pharisee was observed clandestinely making late-night visits to the dwelling place where the Rabbi Jesus was staying.

Marcus continued, afterward Nicodemus appeared to be somewhat transformed, articulating abstract notions of spiritual rebirth and the stark contrast between the realms of darkness and light. Some say he emphasized the dichotomy of evil thriving in the shadows while goodness flourished in the illumination of light. Although this may cause future problems for Nicodemus, he might be the best one to seek intel into Jesus and his followers Passover plans.

Another influential member of the Sanhedrin is a man named Joseph of Arimathea. He is an openly liberal religious leader, much more of a free thinker than others in the Sanhedrin. He must have significant input, as he has his finger on the pulse of Caiaphas more than anyone, as he doesn't want his own thinking to wind up costing his position, or his own life!

Gamaliel was a respected Pharisee and a member of the Sanhedrin. Apparently, he is a Doctor of Jewish Law. He is known for his moderation and wisdom but is a quiet man who doesn't want to ruffle the feathers of the rest of the Sanhedrin, at least publicly! We do believe he advises caution and tolerance toward the this rabbi and his followers.

Another potential insight into Jesus' intentions over the Passover holiday is Simon, a Pharisee and a member of the religious elite, is known for the strict adherence to Jewish laws and traditions. Marcus continued that a couple years ago, it is documented that Simon invited Jesus to dine at his house. The apparent motivation behind this invitation may have been rooted in Simon's desire to engage with the charismatic Rabbi and perhaps assess the nature of his teachings. The dinner apparently took an unexpected turn when a sinful woman entered the scene, anointing Jesus' feet with costly perfume and expressing deep repentance.

So it seems that Simon learned a profound lesson about the boundless nature of forgiveness and the transformative power of genuine repentance. It has been said that this Rabbi Jesus seized the opportunity to teach that the one forgiven much, loves much. That the importance of humility in understanding the depth of divine mercy, apparently challenging the norms of the times that God is a vengeful God. So he might be a great resource to talk with, although we don't believe he has had any further discussions with the Rabbi Jesus or any of his followers.

My First Interview - Caiaphas

Under the bright blue sky of Jerusalem, I found myself standing before the imposing House of Caiaphas, the residence of the high priest and his father-in-law, Annas. The air was thick with the scent of incense, and within the stone walls held the weight of centuries of religious and political intrigue.

With the sun casting long shadows on the cobblestone steps up the hill and the pathway to this magnificent building, I approached the entrance, the heavy door creaking as I entered the dimly lit entrance hall. The servants, with watchful eyes, led me to the presence of Caiaphas and Annas.

The room, adorned with tapestries and symbols of religious authority, bore witness to the grandeur of the priestly elite. Caiaphas and Annas, figures of authority and influence, regarded me with a mix of curiosity and suspicion. As a Roman centurion, I carried the weight of Roman might, and their expressions revealed a tension between the political realities of the time.

"Priests of Jerusalem," I addressed them with a respectful salute, "I am Longinus. I have been sent by Caesar to ensure the peace and stability of this city during the upcoming Passover season. Rumors have reached the ears of Rome regarding a certain Jesus of Nazareth, and I seek your counsel on the matter."

Caiaphas, adorned in ceremonial attire, exchanged a glance with Annas, his father-in-law. The air hung heavy with unspoken tension as I awaited their response. Annas, a figure of considerable influence, spoke with measured words.

"Longinus," he began, "this Jesus is a threat to the established order. His teachings have stirred the people, and the fervor surrounding him could disrupt the harmony we strive to maintain during the sacred Passover festivities."

Caiaphas, his eyes fixed on mine, added, "We have our own ways of dealing with those who challenge the authority bestowed upon us by God. Should Jesus make his way to Jerusalem, the consequences may be dire."

I pressed further, seeking to understand the nuances of their sentiments. "What is it about Jesus that poses such a threat? Is it merely his teachings, or is there a deeper concern?"

Annas, leaning forward, responded, "His influence extends beyond mere words. Magic they all refer to as miracles are attributed to him, and the people are drawn to him as a potential messianic figure. Such false claims challenge our authority and risk destabilizing the delicate balance we maintain with Roman rule."

Caiaphas, with a steely gaze, concluded, "Longinus, be vigilant. The coming days will test the strength of our alliance with not only Pilate, but Ceasar. Rome seeks order, and we seek to maintain the peace under God's guidance. It is in our shared interests to ensure that this Jesus does not disrupt the harmony we've cultivated."

As I exited the House of Caiaphas, the weight of their words lingered. The delicate dance between Roman authority, religious leadership, and the enigmatic figure of Jesus set the stage for a complex and challenging season in Jerusalem.

Less Intense Interviews

The winding streets of Jerusalem led me to the abode of Nicodemus, a Pharisee known for his intellectual pursuits and a degree of curiosity about the teachings of Jesus. The air was filled with a sense of expectancy as I approached his residence, nestled within the heart of the city.

The courtyard of Nicodemus's house exuded an ambiance of scholarly reflection. The scent of parchment mingled with the fragrance of blooming flowers, creating an atmosphere that spoke of both wisdom and contemplation. I entered the abode with a respectful nod to the servants who guided me to Nicodemus.

In the quietude of his study, Nicodemus welcomed me with a warmth that belied the tensions of the time. "Longinus," he greeted, "what brings a Roman centurion to my humble dwelling?"

With a salute, I began, "Nicodemus, I have been dispatched by Caesar to ensure the peace during the Passover season. Rumors of a certain Jesus of Nazareth have reached the ears of Rome, and I seek your insights on the matter. What do you foresee during this festival? What sentiments prevail among the people?"

Nicodemus, known for his measured words, considered the inquiry. "Longinus," he responded, "the city buzzes with anticipation. Jesus is a figure of intrigue. His teachings have sparked conversations in every corner, and the atmosphere is charged with a mix of hope and uncertainty."

As the discussion unfolded, Nicodemus shared his observations on the impact of Jesus' teachings, the diverse reactions among the Pharisees, and the potential implications for the Passover season. His perspective, informed by both intellectual curiosity and a sense of moral duty, offered a nuanced understanding of the complex dynamics at play in Jerusalem.

As I left Nicodemus's dwelling, the weight of his insights resonated. The mosaic of sentiments in Jerusalem painted a complex picture, and the upcoming Passover promised to be a crucible of political and spiritual forces. The streets echoed with the unspoken tension of a city on the brink of transformation.

As the sun dipped below the horizon, casting hues of orange and purple across the Jerusalem skyline, the bustling city began to settle into the quietude of evening. The day's interactions with Caiaphas and Annas, along with the insightful discourse with Nicodemus, left me with much to contemplate. The whispers of political and religious intrigue echoed in my mind, urging me to seek further perspectives.

The aroma of roasting lamb wafted through the air as I entered a local tavern, its warm glow inviting weary travelers and city dwellers alike. Seated at a sturdy wooden table, I beckoned the innkeeper for a hearty meal, a respite from the weight of the day's discussions.

The savory flavors of the meal were a welcome contrast to the complexities of my mission. As I savored each bite, I pondered the tasks that lay ahead. Tomorrow held the promise of conversations with Joseph of Arimathea and Gamaliel, two figures whose perspectives could shed light on the broader strategy of the Jewish leaders in dealing with the potential arrival of Jesus in Jerusalem.

After finishing the meal, I withdrew to a quiet corner, unfurling scrolls and maps on the table. The flickering candlelight danced upon the parchment, casting shadows that mirrored the intricate web of alliances and tensions within the city. Tomorrow's discussions required careful consideration, a delicate dance between diplomacy and the pursuit of critical information.

With a quill in hand, I sketched out a plan of action — a series of questions to unravel the tapestry of strategy that Caiaphas, Annas, and

Nicodemus hinted at but did not fully reveal. The insight from Joseph of Arimathea, a member of the Sanhedrin with a unique perspective, and Gamaliel, known for his wisdom, promised to complete the puzzle.

As the tavern's ambiance shifted from lively chatter to a subdued hum, I folded the parchments, sealing my preparations for tomorrow. The city outside was now veiled in the silence of the night, its secrets and stories echoing through the cobblestone streets. With the strategies laid out before me, I retired to my lodging, ready to navigate the intricate terrain of Jerusalem once again come the light of dawn.

The Second Day of Investigations

The next day unfolded with the sun's gradual ascent, casting its golden glow over the city. I set forth with purpose, the cobbled streets awakening beneath the steady rhythm of my footsteps. The destination was clear – conversations awaited with Joseph of Arimathea and Gamaliel, key figures whose perspectives held the potential to illuminate the intricacies of Jerusalem's political and religious landscape.

Navigating the mazelike pathways, I arrived at the residence of Joseph of Arimathea. The air carried a certain gravity as I approached, for this man, a member of the Sanhedrin, was known for his allegiance to both the Jewish council and apparently a concealed sympathy for Jesus.

The door creaked open, and Joseph welcomed me into his abode. We engaged in a dialogue that traversed the realms of duty, faith, and the delicate balance he maintained within the religious hierarchy. His insights provided a valuable piece of the puzzle, hinting at the underlying tensions within the Sanhedrin.

With the weight of newfound knowledge, I proceeded to the revered halls of learning where Gamaliel, an esteemed Pharisee, had the ability to exert power and influence. The scholarly atmosphere resonated with the echoes of ancient wisdom as I entered his presence.

Our discourse ranged from the prophecies of old to the currents of dissent within Jerusalem. Gamaliel, a voice of moderation, shared his concerns about potential uprisings and the delicate equilibrium between Roman rule and the Jewish identity.

As the day progressed, the pieces of information gleaned from Joseph of Arimathea and Gamaliel began to converge. The strategy of the Jewish leaders unfolded before me – a nuanced dance between maintaining religious order, appeasing Roman authorities, and quelling the fervor surrounding Jesus of Nazareth.

The sun dipped once more, casting elongated shadows across the city. Reflecting on the day's conversations, I retraced my steps through the labyrinth of walkways of Jerusalem, armed with a more comprehensive understanding of the forces at play.

The tapestry of alliances and rivalries within the city was now clearer, yet shadows lingered on the edges of this revelation. As I retired for the night, the city below embraced the silence, holding its secrets close. Tomorrow promised further challenges and revelations as I navigated the intricate currents of Jerusalem, seeking to unravel the mysteries of Jesus and the delicate balance between Roman might and religious authority.

Seeking Balanced Input

The night hung heavy with unanswered questions, and my restless slumber offered no solace. Tossing and turning on the coarse bed, my mind grappled with the enigma that was Jesus of Nazareth. Why did his mere presence stir the hearts and place anger in the minds of the Jewish leaders? What power did he hold that could potentially disrupt the delicate peace of Jerusalem?

As the first light of dawn painted the horizon, I rose from the troubled sleep, a weariness etched into every fiber of my being. The city below, still wrapped in the quiet of predawn, seemed to hold its collective breath, awaiting the unfolding of another day of intrigue.

The echoes of my footsteps through the narrow alleys became a rhythmic companion as I traversed the streets, contemplating the task at hand. If understanding was to be gained, it required proximity to the source – Jesus or one of his followers. But finding him amidst the labyrinth of Jerusalem proved a formidable challenge. I might need to go beyond the gates for answers.

My inquiries led me to the quarters where rumors hinted at gatherings of Jesus' followers. The clandestine nature of their meetings spoke volumes about the heightened tensions that surrounded this charismatic figure. The air was charged with anticipation as I approached, the atmosphere pregnant with the possibility of encountering those who pledged allegiance to Jesus.

I engaged in conversations with the locals, discreetly probing for information that could guide me to this elusive figure. Whispers of miracles, teachings, and gatherings in obscure corners of the city lingered in the air. It became evident that Jesus had woven a tapestry of followers whose fervor was matched only by the intrigue surrounding their leader.

The day unfolded with a meticulous pursuit, an intricate dance through the alleys and marketplaces of Jerusalem. My interactions with the people, however, left me with a mosaic of impressions – admiration, skepticism, fear. The multifaceted responses to Jesus painted a picture of a man whose influence transcended the boundaries of comprehension.

As the sun descended once more, painting the city in hues of amber and rose, I found myself at the crossroads of decision. The pursuit of Jesus, an mysterious figure with the potential to disrupt the peace, became a mission that transcended the bounds of duty. The unraveling of the mystery would demand not only perseverance but a delicate dance between the political currents and the fervent undercurrents of faith in Jerusalem.

Under the cloak of night, with the city shrouded in shadows, I made my way to the upper city. The hill rose before me, crowned by the residence of Joseph of Arimathea. The air was crisp with a sense of secrecy, each footfall echoing the weight of the questions that pressed upon me.

Arriving at the crest, I navigated the quiet pathways until the imposing structure came into view. The large room above Joseph's home, where Jesus' followers purportedly gathered in secret, loomed as a haven of clandestine discussions.

A subtle knock, barely audible in the stillness of the night, brought Joseph to the door. His eyes bore the weariness of one burdened by both duty and conviction. "Longinus," he acknowledged with a nod, inviting me into the discreet quarters.

In the dimly lit room, surrounded by the hushed tones of those gathered, I broached the subject with Joseph. "I've heard whispers of meetings here," I began, choosing my words carefully. "What transpires in these clandestine discussions, and what are the true intentions of this Jesus of Nazareth?"

Joseph, a man of both faith and discernment, met my gaze with a measured look. "These meetings are but reflections of a deep yearning for understanding," he replied, his words carrying the weight of sincerity. "Jesus' teachings have ignited a fervor, a hunger for spiritual truths that transcend the norms of our time."

As the night unfolded, Joseph shared insights into the gatherings. The followers of Jesus sought to comprehend a message that challenged the status quo, and their secrecy was born not out of rebellion but out of caution. Caution against the very powers that sought to maintain order, like the one I represented.

I posed pointed questions about the intentions of Jesus and the potential for unrest. Joseph's responses presented a detailed and intricate picture — a leader whose intentions were rooted in a spiritual awakening rather than political upheaval. The teachings, discussions, and debates in that room were an exploration of profound truths rather than a conspiracy against the established order.

My clandestine conversations with Joseph of Arimathea unraveled the mystery surrounding the secretive gatherings. The complexities of Jesus' influence, far from a mere challenge to the status quo, spoke to the deep spiritual hunger within the hearts of those who sought enlightenment in the shadows of the upper city.

As I departed, the moon casting a silvery glow over Jerusalem, I carried with me a more nuanced understanding. The journey to unravel the enigma of Jesus continued, each clandestine meeting, each whispered conversation, peeling away layers of the mystery that surrounded this charismatic figure.

Who Was The God Of Israel?

Dawn broke over Jerusalem, painting the city in hues of gold and amber. Yet, as the first light pierced through my window, I awoke to a perplexing revelation that lingered from the depths of the night. The God of the Jews, a deity shrouded in centuries of mystery, provoked a bewildering curiosity within me.

As I rose from a restless sleep, my thoughts swirled in the labyrinth of questions. How did this belief endure through generations, binding the people of Israel to a set of rules and rituals? A God whose presence seemed elusive, veiled in the echoes of prophets and the pages of sacred scrolls.

My musings led me back through the annals of history, where only a handful claimed to have witnessed the divine. Moses on Mount Sinai, a burning bush that spoke the words of God. Prophets who glimpsed visions and spoke of encounters with the Almighty. Yet, the tangible presence of this deity remained elusive to the masses.

I pondered the paradox — a people devoted to a God they feared. A God whose commandments formed the pillars of their existence, yet whose face remained veiled in the mysteries of the divine. How did faith persist, unwavering, through generations, fueled by the promise of a messiah, an anointed one who would usher in a new era?

The narratives of patriarchs, judges, and kings unfolded in my mind, each chapter a testament to a covenant with this enigmatic deity. The temple rituals, the sacrifices, the intricate web of laws — all woven into the fabric of a belief system that dictated every aspect of life.

In the silence of my chamber, I grappled with the essence of this God, revered and feared. The profound faith of the Jews, resilient through conquests and exiles, resonated with a tenacity that defied reason. A God whose presence transcended the tangible, whose mysteries beckoned the seeker and confounded the skeptic.

As the day unfolded, I traveled to be immersed in the streets of nearby Bethlehem, observing the devout as they engaged in rituals, adhering to a set of commandments that dictated their every step. The palpable reverence for a God they could not see, a God whose voice echoed only through prophets and resonated in the sacred texts, left me in a state of both fascination and bemusement.

The journey to unravel the intricacies of the Jewish faith, intertwined with the unfolding drama of Jesus of Nazareth, had opened a gateway to a world where the divine and the earthly collided. As I navigated the city, the perplexing tapestry of beliefs and rituals stretched before me, inviting me to explore the depths of a faith that endured through epochs, a faith bound to a God whose essence remained a profound mystery.

The perplexing path of my contemplation now led me to the crux of the matter — Jesus of Nazareth. If, indeed, he was proclaimed as the Son of God, why did he choose to enter this world in such humble circumstances? Why would, in Bethlehem, a town of modest repute, bore witness to the birth of a child destined to alter the course of history.

The narrative unfolded in my mind — Joseph, the carpenter, and Mary, a peasant girl. The whispers of scandal surrounding Mary's pregnancy before the marriage was consummated stirred doubts within the community. A fledgling family, pursued by the shadows of gossip and judgment, conveniently left Nazareth for the census, had the child, then fled to Egypt in fear of Herod's wrath.

The questions persisted, weaving a fabric of uncertainty. Why would the Son of God, the bearer of divine grace, emerge into the world through such humble origins? Did he not deserve a grand entrance, a heralding of celestial trumpets and celestial splendor? Why Bethlehem, a town that echoed with simplicity rather than the grandeur befitting a divine being?

As I walked the streets, the echoes of Bethlehem whispered tales of shepherds, wise men, and a lowly manger. The irreconcilability lingered — a child born to Joseph, a carpenter, and Mary, a woman whose conception sparked whispers of scandal. Yet, the air carried stories of miracles, healings, and teachings that transcended the ordinary.

The discrepancy of the narrative gnawed at my understanding. The Son of God choosing an earthly existence that defied the expectations of celestial splendor. Was this deliberate humility, a divine paradox meant to confound the wisdom of mortals? The flight to Egypt, the clandestine departure, the shroud of mystery — it all seemed to form a tapestry woven with threads of enigma.

As the sun dipped below the horizon, casting shadows upon Bethlehem's humble streets, I grappled with the complexities of divine incarnation. The questions lingered, demanding answers that eluded reason. If Jesus truly bore the divine mantle, the circumstances of his birth seemed like an intentional veil, obscuring the grandeur one might expect.

The journey into the heart of this mystery, where the divine intersected with the mundane, invited me to traverse uncharted territories of faith and understanding. As the night settled over Bethlehem, the stars above bore silent witness to the enigma of a child born in a stable, whose destiny intertwined with the very fabric of humanity's salvation.

The enigma of Jesus deepened as I pondered the threads of his teachings, the wonders that unfolded in the quiet corners and bustling streets alike. Small groups spoke of intimate gatherings where Jesus illuminated the path of love — love for one another and a Father in heaven. These were the teachings that echoed through the ages, carrying the weight of a profound simplicity that resonated even with those who doubted.

The tales of healings, witnessed by small clusters and vast crowds alike, painted a portrait of a man whose touch could mend the broken and restore sight to the blind. Hundreds bore witness to miracles that transcended the boundaries of earthly understanding. Lame walked, blind saw, and the sick were made whole by a power that defied the natural order.

Yet, as I contemplated these wonders, the complexities of belief unfolded. The teachings centered on love, compassion, and a Father in heaven. A heaven — a place that seemed distant, shrouded in the unknown. Where was this heavenly realm, and how did Jesus' Father ascend to such ethereal heights?

The questions multiplied, each one a labyrinth leading into the depths of theological uncertainty. The Jews, who staunchly held to their beliefs, asserted that Jesus' teachings were not of their own tradition. And yet, Jesus stood as a Rabbi, a figure entwined with the fabric of Judaism. The dichotomy of faiths, the confusion that danced on the edges of comprehension, perplexed the very essence of my understanding.

In the quiet moments of reflection, I grappled with the paradoxes. If Jesus' teachings were rooted in love and compassion, why did they stir such discord among the established order? The very fabric of heaven and the nature of divinity seemed elusive, like veiled mysteries awaiting revelation.

The night in Bethlehem embraced my contemplation, and the stars overhead seemed to witness the wrestling of mortal understanding with the ineffable. The journey into the heart of faith, a path trodden by believers and skeptics alike, invited me to navigate the intricacies of a belief system that defied the bounds of reason.

As I walked the cobbled streets, the teachings of Jesus lingered — love for one another, compassion for the downtrodden, and a Father in heaven whose nature eluded my grasp. The paradoxes unfolded like petals of an enigmatic flower, inviting me to explore the very essence of belief that echoed through the ages, challenging the boundaries of earthly wisdom.

Anointing of a King?

The air, back in my chamber stirred as the scout, weary from the journey, delivered his report. His assignment was clear — seek out Jesus of Nazareth, observe his actions, document his teachings. The scout's eyes, wide with intrigue, conveyed the weight of revelations that awaited.

"In Bethany," the scout began, "I found him reclining at a meal, surrounded by followers and curious onlookers. The atmosphere was charged with anticipation. A woman named Mary approached, bearing a vial of incredibly expensive oil."

As the scout unfolded the scene, my mind grappled with the significance of this act. Anointing, a ritual reserved for kings and nobility, whispered tales of royal consecrations throughout history. The oil, a symbol of prosperity, blessings, and stability, dripped onto the hair and feet of Jesus, an act that transcended mere symbolism.

"The use of anointing oils," the scout continued, "is varied among the Jews. It could signify cleansing, prepare for transportable temples, or denote prosperity. However, there's more — it's also a means of healing or preparation for burial."

Perplexity crept into the room. Was Jesus orchestrating a regal ascent, preparing for a role that defied the expectations of the Roman order? The possibilities hung in the air, an unspoken tension between the rituals of anointing and the political ramifications that might follow.

"Was this an act of preparation for some insurrection in Jerusalem?" I questioned; my thoughts vocalized. "Could he be a potential threat not just to the Jews but to Caesar himself?"

The scout nodded, mirroring the uncertainty that danced in my mind. The enigma of Jesus deepened with each revelation, and the rituals that unfolded seemed to blur the lines between divine reverence and political subversion.

The night pressed on; my mind entangled in a web of conjecture. As I looked out over the moonlit city, the whispers of Bethany echoed — anointing oil, a potent symbol overflowing with potential meanings. The journey to unravel the mysteries of Jesus of Nazareth had taken an unexpected turn, veering into realms where faith and politics converged, leaving me to navigate the shadows of uncertainty that lingered on the horizon.

The scout's narrative unfolded like an intricate tapestry, weaving a tale that traversed from Bethany to Perea, beyond the Jordan, where the belief in Jesus ripened among the people. It continued near the border between Samaria and Galilee, where a profound event defied the realms of the conceivable.

"Beyond the Jordan," the scout recounted, "he stood near the border, where ten lepers approached him, defying the orders to keep a safe distance. Astonishingly, he ministered to them, providing healing words that transcended the boundaries of conventional understanding."

The revelation hung in the air, laden with incredulity. How could one defy the strictures of contagion and minister to those deemed untouchable? The scout continued, "As they walked away, a miraculous transformation unfolded. The sores of leprosy, like scales shedding from their bodies, fell away, leaving them cleansed."

The perplexity etched itself onto my expression. Leprosy, a scourge that marked one as an outcast, defied not only the laws of the physical world but the societal norms as well. The scout's account painted a portrait of a healer whose actions transcended the boundaries of earthly comprehension.

"Could such a transformation be possible?" I questioned, a rhetorical inquiry that hung in the room. The scout, too, seemed to wrestle with the implausibility of the scene he witnessed near the border between Samaria and Galilee.

The night pressed on, the celestial expanse above bearing silent witness to the unfolding mysteries. The narrative of Jesus of Nazareth, a healer who defied the confines of maladies deemed incurable, added yet another layer to the perplexities that surrounded him.

As I contemplated the scout's words, the question lingered — how could one man wield such transformative power, challenging not only the physical ailments but the societal norms that dictated the boundaries between the clean and the unclean? The journey to understand Jesus of Nazareth took me further into the realms where the miraculous and the inexplicable converged, leaving me to navigate the shadows of wonder and uncertainty that surrounded this enigmatic figure.

The scout's report now veered into the realm of parables, and the story of talents unfolded like an enigmatic scroll before my mind. As Jesus headed back toward Jerusalem, he spoke to the crowd, weaving a narrative about entrusting different individuals with varying amounts of talents to invest on his behalf. The ones who invested wisely were rewarded proportionally.

The layers of meaning in this tale hung in the air, inviting speculation and interpretation. As the scout conveyed the narrative, my mind grappled with the possibilities. Could this be a coded message, a subtle call to action? Was Jesus implying that those who invested their efforts wisely, perhaps in supporting a movement against the Jewish leaders or even the Roman Empire, would be rewarded?

The complexities of the parable echoed through my thoughts. The notion of investment, reward, and wise stewardship seemed to resonate not only in the economic sense but also in the political and social spheres. Was this a veiled message about a potential uprising or a call for allegiance to a cause beyond the immediate understanding?

"Could it be," I pondered aloud, "that within the context of the Jewish faith, there's a deeper meaning to this parable? Perhaps a metaphorical representation of spiritual investments, where the return is not material wealth but divine favor?"

The scout, attuned to the layers of intrigue that surrounded Jesus' teachings, nodded in contemplation. The parables of Jesus, it seemed, were not merely stories but cryptic narratives that invited reflection and interpretation. The journey to decipher their true meanings led through a labyrinth of possibilities.

The night enveloped us, and the city beyond the window slumbered in shadows. The tale of talents lingered in my mind, a cipher with implications that extended beyond the immediate narrative. The enigma of Jesus' messages, the potential for hidden meanings, fueled the quest to unravel the complexities of this charismatic figure and the path he beckoned his followers to tread.

The Procession Begins

News of the procession from Bethany to Bethphage, with Jesus and Lazarus leading the way, reached me like a whisper in the wind. The setting, the narrow road winding up the Mount of Olives, conjured a scene of profound symbolism.

"Why this procession, and what message does Jesus seek to convey?" I pondered, my thoughts lingering on the significance of the chosen path. The journey from Bethany, a place where Lazarus had risen from the grave, where he laid 4 days to Bethphage, perched atop the Mount of Olives, felt full of intentional symbolism.

First, when Jesus mourned over the death of his good friend Lazarus, he wanted to raise him, even though Lazarus' sister begged him to leave her brother in the tomb, first because after 4 days, "there would surely be a stench" and secondly, maybe because she lacked the faith that Jesus would be successful, for her love for Jesus was greater than her faith that he could command life after death.

This, to me was so strange that Martha might lack the faith in Jesus. I turned to Joseph of Arimathea, who was standing near me, to ask this question. He said that Lazarus and his sisters Mary and Martha often came to his house with the others to discuss the meaning within the scrolls and how Jesus' teaching across Galilee brought a deeper, more fulfilling meaning to the words on the scrolls. But even them, Martha was often tending to the needs of the gatherings, such as filling the glasses with water, wine or bringing fragments of bread for all of us to nibble on. Both Lazarus and Mary were the ones full of faith, always paying attention to the dialog, and as some may say, they chose the better part. Martha was there and served, but her faith life was not that deep.

As Jesus and Lazarus led the way, a spectacle of divine power and resurrection unfolded. Lazarus, once entombed, now walked among the living, a testament to the miraculous capabilities attributed to Jesus. The crowd followed, a tapestry of disciples, Martha, Mary — witnesses to the extraordinary event that defied the natural order.

The question lingered — what could Jesus be aiming to prove with this procession? Was it a public declaration of his divine authority, a manifestation of power over life and death? The Mount of Olives, with its historical and prophetic significance, seemed to amplify the weight of the moment.

"Is he proclaiming kingship or messiahship?" I mused, contemplating the political undercurrents that might ripple through Jerusalem at the sight of such a procession. The symbolism of Jesus and Lazarus leading the way carried echoes of a leader and a follower, a narrative that could be interpreted in various ways.

As the crowd ascended the Mount of Olives, my thoughts gravitated toward the disciples, Martha, and Mary — witnesses to Lazarus' resurrection and the unfolding events. What emotions stirred within them? Did they see this procession as a triumphant proclamation or as a precursor to unforeseen challenges? The quest to comprehend the deeper meaning behind this procession lingered, a puzzle whose pieces awaited revelation.

The significance of this event, the motives that propelled such a gathering, stirred questions within me. Why did Jesus, with Lazarus at his side, embark on this symbolic journey?

The procession wound its way from Bethany, nestled on the eastern slope of the Mount of Olives, toward Bethphage at its summit. Martha and Mary, sisters of Lazarus, and Jesus' close disciples followed, creating a spectacle that drew attention and curiosity.

If there was going to be an opportunity for a clash between the Jewish Leaders in Jerusalem and Jesus of Nazareth and his followers, this might be it! I sent my scout to Pilate's Palace to share the news of this procession and to ask Pilate to release the 80 men I brought with me to meet me at the area inside the Golden Gate, and send another detail to the areas around the Temple, just in case.

As the hours passed, the scene unfolded with Jesus riding a donkey, a deliberate choice laden with symbolism. The donkey, a creature associated with peace and meekness, stood in stark contrast to the warlike connotations of a horse. I couldn't help but contemplate the deliberate intent behind such a choice, but I was ready with my detail of men from Rome.

The Jews I inquired with mentioned a prophecy from the Book of Zechariah — "Behold, your king is coming to you, humble and mounted on a donkey." The realization that Jesus might be intentionally fulfilling a prophetic declaration added layers of complexity to the unfolding narrative.

"How," I wondered, "could Jesus become a king through such a peaceful and humble manner?" The juxtaposition between traditional notions of kingship, marked by power and might, and Jesus' deliberate choice of humility and peace, left me pondering the motives behind this symbolic journey.

The symbolism of Jesus' impending peaceful entrance, a fulfillment of prophecy, cast shadows of uncertainty. The journey to understand the motivations behind this calculated display continued, each step raising questions about the nature of leadership and the path Jesus envisioned for himself and his followers.

As the news spread of Jesus entering Jerusalem through The Golden Gate, my curiosity led me to witness the scene from a closer vantage point. I made my way toward where I sent my men, very near the gate. The air buzzed with anticipation as a crowd gathered, stretched out their necks to catch a glimpse of the unfolding spectacle.

The significance of this entrance wasn't lost on me. The Jews I encountered spoke of The Golden Gate as 'The Gate of Mercy' (Sha'ar HaRachamim), a place intricately woven into their beliefs. In Jewish tradition, it was considered the portal from which the Messiah would enter in the end of days. Others call the Golden Gate the "Gate of Redemption". Although I believe the terms to be somewhat interchangeable, to me, redemption is something you seek, mercy is something you are granted. In any case, the convergence of belief and the unfolding events added a layer of intrigue to the already charged atmosphere.

As I observed, the area inside the gate teemed with people, their faces alight with excitement. They held palm branches, a symbol that resonated deeply within Jewish traditions. The air pulsated with the rhythmic chant of "Hosanna in the highest!" Each echo seemed to carry with it a resonance of fervent expectation and hope.

The symbolism of palm branches, a sign of victory and peace, intertwined with the cries of "Hosanna," echoed through the ages. It wasn't lost on me that this event might hold profound significance beyond the immediate spectacle. The convergence of Jesus entering through The Golden Gate, the crowd's jubilant praise, and the symbolism embedded in their actions left me pondering the depths of their beliefs.

"What might this mean?" I mused, contemplating the unfolding drama. The crowd's fervor, the use of palm branches, and the chant of "Hosanna" seemed to convey a belief in Jesus as a figure of triumph and deliverance. The resonance with messianic expectations painted the scene with layers of anticipation and hope.

Even I got caught up in the jubilation of the people, with echoes of "Hosanna in the highest" lingering in my ears. The Golden Gate, a silent witness to the procession, stood as a threshold between the present and the prophetic future, as there was no resistance from the Jewish Leaders, which greatly pleased me. The journey to understand the implications of this moment, rich with symbolism and belief, continued, each step unraveling the tapestry of faith and expectation woven within the walls of Jerusalem.

Tables Turned

The day continued to unfolded with details I missed as Jesus returned to Jerusalem on the donkey. I found that along the way, Jesus, in a seemingly inexplicable act, cursed a fig tree that had failed to bear fruit. The symbolism of this gesture lingered in my thoughts — was it a representation of judgment on the religious leaders, an indictment of their failure to cultivate true, living faith that bears spiritual fruit? Was this a gesture of potential reason for action within his followers?

My men and I, curious as to what would happen next followed behind the procession. I had requested that Pilate assign a detail of men at the temple area, so if they were there, with me and my men behind the procession, we could quickly stop any upheaval within the procession. The journey continued, and as we arrived at the Temple, the scene transformed into a tumult of activity. The temple courts, intended for prayer and reverence, were marred by the presence of corrupt money changers. Jesus, fueled by righteous anger, did not hold back. I watched, a silent observer, as he overturned tables and drove out those who had turned the sacred space into a den of thieves. I heard Jesus declare "My Temple will be a house of prayer, but you have turned it into a den of thieves." The weight of those words resonated through the air, confronting the corruption that had taken root within the sacred precincts. Most of the people just stood and watched, in silent protest to the disgust they had that the Jewish Leaders allow to happen within their temple.

We were there to keep the peace. With the rebellion being one sided, Jesus being the only one causing any damage, we had no role in this matter, so I refrained from interference, recognizing that this was a situation best addressed by the religious leaders. The complexities of the Temple's administration and the corruption within its walls were matters that required internal resolution. As a Roman centurion, my role was to maintain order, and in this instance, the intervention of the religious authorities seemed more appropriate.

In this time of observation, I meditated on how some of the people passed through the Gate of Repentance side of the Golden Gate, yet when they went to the temple seeking forgiveness for their bad ways bought doves, small animals like sheep or goats to offer for their own sins. It distressed me to think that it was acceptable to use your money to purchase an animal to die for your own sins. And the money spent to purchase the animals – did that go to the farmers who raised the animals or to the Temple leaders?

The day wore on, and the echoes of Jesus' actions reverberated within the Temple. The cleansing, though disruptive, seemed to carry a call to the same accountability that I had just been thinking. The juxtaposition of the cursing of the fig tree and the cleansing of the Temple invited contemplation — a commentary on the need for genuine, fruitful faith and the responsibility of those entrusted with spiritual leadership.

As I observed from the periphery, the narrative unfolded with layers of symbolism and challenge. The path Jesus treaded, fraught with confrontation and symbolic gestures, left me grappling with the complexities of faith, judgment, and the need for integrity within religious institutions. The journey to understand the motivations and implications of these events continued, each step marked by the unfolding drama within the heart of Jerusalem. These thoughts were very different from the issues I had to deal with in Rome!

What could I do... what should I do, with the observations I just witnessed? Then I noticed how Jesus went to the far end of the temple and sat on a step. The large group had begun to dissipate but those left were cripples and the lame, for they were there begging for money and food and could not leave with the rest of the crowd or they might get trampled. It was at that end of the temple where Jesus rested on the steps.

From a distance, we witnessed that after he talked with them, he moved from step to step, touching a leg of one man, an arm of the other, a foot of a woman and so many more with great obvious physical impairments. Each leaped up and screamed "Hosanna" for they were cured. It was clear that whatever they sought from this man, Jesus, they received Mercy. Great Mercy.

The Destruction Of Jerusalem

It was then midweek and the unfolding events in Jerusalem continued on this new day, Wednesday. My scout said that the city's atmosphere carried an undercurrent of tension and conflict. Jesus and his disciples returned to the city, where the religious leaders had laid a trap to arrest him. However, Jesus, seemingly elusive and undeterred, managed to evade their snares. Instead, he pronounced harsh judgments upon them, using potent imagery to highlight their hypocrisy and inner corruption.

"Blind guides!" Jesus declared. "You are like whitewashed tombs—beautiful on the outside but filled on the inside with dead people's bones and all sorts of impurity. Outwardly you look like righteous people, but inwardly your hearts are filled with hypocrisy and lawlessness. Snakes! Sons of vipers! How will you escape the judgment of hell?"

The scout's report painted a picture of confrontations and condemnations, leaving me to ponder the motivations behind Jesus' taunts. The sharp words, a scathing rebuke of the religious leaders, seemed to escalate the tension within the already charged atmosphere of Jerusalem. What was the motivation he had to provoke them like this? This seemed like his own personal crusade against the religious leaders. Although he often had a pack of followers with him, they rarely seemed to talk. Were they the smart ones or cowards?

Later in the afternoon, my scout reported that Jesus and his disciples withdrew from the city to the Mount of Olives. There, overlooking Jerusalem, Jesus delivered an elaborate prophecy about the destruction of the city and the end of the age. He spoke of his return and a final judgment that would unfold.

The weight of these statements hung in the air, and my thoughts drifted toward the implications. What did Jesus mean by the destruction of Jerusalem, the end of the age, and a final judgment? The gravity of these prophecies left me apprehensive about the potential impact on the already fragile peace in Jerusalem.

The responsibility to maintain order and peace in the city weighed heavily on my shoulders. How could I navigate the intricacies of this situation, where spiritual tensions collided with political and social dynamics? The convergence of religious fervor, prophecy, and potential unrest loomed ahead, presenting a complex challenge in my mission to keep the peace in Jerusalem.

Then I learned of the revelation that one of Jesus' close disciples, Judas, had met with the Sanhedrin and offered to lead them to Jesus in exchange for silver coins, adding a new layer of complexity to the unfolding drama. The motives behind Judas' actions remained a puzzle, and the implications of this betrayal stirred a mix of concern and speculation within me.

Could this be the end of the entire situation, a resolution to the tension that had been escalating in Jerusalem? Or was it a strategic move, another twist in the narrative designed to confound the religious leaders and those who sought Jesus' arrest?

The ambiguity of the situation left me grappling with uncertainty. Judas, apparently a trusted disciple and the group's treasurer, taking such a drastic step raised questions about the internal dynamics within Jesus' circle and the motivations that might drive someone to betray their leader. The intricate interplay of loyalty, personal motives, and the broader political and religious context added complexity to the already convoluted series of events.

As I pondered the implications, the fragility of the peace I sought to maintain in Jerusalem became even more apparent. The potential for betrayal from within Jesus' inner circle introduced an element of unpredictability, challenging my ability to navigate the intricate threads of loyalty and betrayal that wove through the city. The unfolding drama carried a weight of uncertainty, and I prepared myself for the inevitable challenges that lay ahead in the quest to keep the peace amidst the tumultuous events surrounding Jesus and his disciples.

The Planning Event

The quietness of Wednesday left an air of anticipation, with uncertainty lingering about whether Jesus and his followers deemed the tension too high for an assault on Jerusalem or if strategic planning was underway. The pause in visible activity fueled speculation about the next moves in this intricate dance between religious fervor and political realities.

Then, on Thursday morning, the scout's report unveiled a development — Peter and John were observed heading to the Upper Room above Joseph of Arimathea's house. The purpose behind their visit became a subject of conjecture. Were they making preparations for the upcoming Passover Feast, seeking a respite from the heightened tension, or perhaps plotting their next move from within the gates?

As the day unfolded, Jesus and all of his close disciples, along with family members, arrived at the Upper Room. Joseph and his wife joined them shortly after. The presence of Joseph, a figure with affiliations both within the Jewish leadership and potentially sympathetic to Jesus, raised questions about his role and allegiance.

I found myself wondering whether Joseph might be a spy for the Jewish leaders, gathering intelligence on Jesus and his followers, or if his involvement hinted at a more covert alliance with Jesus. The intricacies of this situation blurred the lines between loyalty and espionage, leaving room for speculation and suspicion to fester.

The Upper Room, a setting which now became a stage where alliances and strategies unfolded. The air was full with unspoken intentions, and I braced myself for the challenges that would inevitably arise. As the events within the Upper Room played out, my job as the centurion charged with keeping the peace, grappled with the complexities of deciphering allegiances and motivations in a city poised on the precipice of tumultuous change.

Captured

The scout's report unfolded with a solemn tone, painting a vivid picture of the events that transpired in the Garden of Gethsemane. Jesus and his disciples left the Upper Room and crossed the Kidron Valley to reach the garden, situated at the base of the Mount of Olives. The anticipation in the air was palpable as the scout recounted that Jesus walked a short distance away from his disciples, who appeared to have fallen asleep.

In the quietude of the garden, Jesus dropped to his knees, leaning on a large boulder, and engaged in intense prayer. The scout, unable to hear the words of his prayer, reported that his movements conveyed the weight of the moment, capturing the essence of Jesus' fervent communion with his father.

The tranquility was shattered when Judas Iscariot led a contingent of temple guards to the location with chains and torches. The arrest unfolded, and Jesus was taken to the home of Caiaphas, the High Priest, where the whole council had gathered to build their case against him.

The scout noted a detail that added a layer of mystery to the unfolding narrative – massive amounts of fresh blood on the rock where Jesus had prayed. The significance of this detail eluded understanding at the moment, leaving an air of bewilderment.

Another somber note emerged as the scout reported that the disciples, in the face of imminent danger, fearfully ran away. The bonds that held them together seemed to fracture in the crucible of this momentous event.

Later, Peter, the main disciple, was spotted in the courtyard of Caiaphas, near a warming fire. Recognition cast a spotlight on him, but in a moment of apparent weakness, he cowardly denied knowing Jesus. This betrayal unfolded just as the sun rose over the hill, marking a stark contrast between the dawn of a new day and the unfolding tragedy.

The scout's report left me pondering the significance of these events. The arrest of Jesus, the scattering of his disciples, and the denial by Peter signaled a dramatic turn. The future of this enigmatic movement hung in the balance as the sun illuminated a city grappling with the weight of its own history and destiny.

Brutality Unleashed

The early hours of Friday abruptly roused me from sleep as commotion echoed through Pilate's courtyard. The Jews had hastily conducted a trial, declaring Jesus guilty of blasphemy. Their authority fell short when it came to the death sentence – a power only Pilate possessed.

Without delay, I descended the steps to the courtyard. My presence served a dual purpose: to observe the unfolding situation and to ensure it remained within manageable and safe bounds. The intersection of religious fervor and Roman governance played out before my watchful eyes.

After a brief discussion with Pilate, Jesus was led away to endure the brutal act of scourging. Duty compelled me to follow – to witness the unfolding tragedy that awaited him. The Roman scourging, known for its unrelenting severity, opened up before me.

The scene was nothing short of gruesome, even for me, a seasoned warrior. The sounds of the scourging, the anguished cries, and the sheer brutality of the act etched themselves into my memory. As a witness to this harrowing event, I grappled with the collision of authority, justice, and the stark brutality wielded in the name of Roman governance.

The events of that Friday morning would forever leave an indelible mark on my consciousness. The delicate equilibrium between religious convictions and imperial power teetered on the precipice of chaos. Navigating the complexities of a city poised on the brink of unrest became my ongoing challenge, as the collision of faith and governance unfolded in the heart of Jerusalem.

I couldn't shake the feeling that compelled me to follow the guards as they dragged Jesus, battered and nearly lifeless, into a cell beneath the palace courtyard. The weight of the moment pressed upon me, and a sense of urgency propelled me to take action.

Approaching the guards stationed outside the locked cell, I asserted my authority, commanding them to leave. The flickering torchlight painted a scene of anticipation and uncertainty as I stood alone outside Jesus' cell.

In the dim, musty confines of the cell, the cold walls seemed to bear witness to the echoes of my own internal turmoil. Bending down to the blood-stained floor, I met his gaze. His eyes, despite the brutality inflicted upon him, held a depth that stirred something within me. In that solemn moment, I spoke to him for the first time, a conversation veiled in shadows and echoes.

"I can speak to Pilate," I offered, my voice a hushed murmur in the dimly lit corridor. "I can convince him to spare you from crucifixion. All you need to do is say you'll take your friends and go back to Galilee and never return. My mission here is to keep peace."

Gathering in all that I saw in his eyes, I could imagine the feel the weight of the whip in my hands, hear the lash of its leather against flesh, the smell of the metallic tang of blood lingering in the air. It was an all too familiar scene for one accustomed to the harsh realities of Roman justice. But this, this was different.

He laid there, stoic yet serene, his gaze looking as if I was not even there, eyes fixed on a point beyond even the cold, unforgiving stone. The flickering torchlight danced upon his face, casting shadows that played across the lines etched by suffering. I, Longinus, the centurion, found myself in the company of a man like no other - Jesus of Nazareth.

As I grappled with the weight of what I had witnessed – the brutality he endured, the mockery of a crown woven from thorns pressed into his brow – he spoke with a calm authority that cut through the oppressive silence of the cell. His eyes met mine, and in that gaze, I sensed a depth of understanding that transcended mortal comprehension.

"Longinus," he began, his voice a quiet but resolute melody in the stillness. "I carry the sin of the world upon my shoulders. Every transgression, every betrayal, every cruelty ever committed and yet to be committed – I bear them all today."

His words hung heavy in the air, each syllable carrying the weight of an entire cosmos of human failings. I couldn't fathom how one man could shoulder such a burden willingly. "Why?" I questioned, the word escaping my lips before I could restrain it.

He spoke not in defense, but in revelation. "My mission is to conquer sin through my death and conquer death by rising again. Through this sacrifice, a pathway to redemption is laid bare for all who believe and seek reconciliation. The shackles of sin, the chains of mortality – broken – as of today!"

In that confined space, his words echoed like a promise, a proclamation that rose above the confines of the cell. I felt the gravity of his mission, the magnitude of a purpose that surpassed the realms of human understanding. And as I looked face to face with this enigmatic figure, I couldn't escape the realization that I, too, stood at the threshold of a profound choice – to witness and comprehend the unfolding of divine purpose or to remain bound by the limitations of mortal comprehension.

In an act of defiance against my offer, although strangely I understood, Jesus gripped the bars of his cell and stood upright. The strength he exuded, despite his battered state, spoke volumes about a kingdom beyond the realm of earthly power struggles.

The torchlight danced on the bars, casting shadows that seemed to waver between the physical and the metaphysical. In that moment, I grappled with the realization that the forces at play went beyond my comprehension. The encounter with Jesus left me standing alone in the quiet corridor, surrounded by the weight of choices and destinies converging in the shadows beneath the palace courtyard.

The End, Or Was It?

It was Friday mid-morning. As I walked behind the procession from the Governor's Palace, the weight of the moment pressed upon me, echoing in every step that followed Jesus along the path to Golgotha. The air was thick with a somber silence, interrupted only by the muffled sobs of those who watched, and the harsh echo of footsteps against the cobbled streets.

Jesus, burdened by the heavy crossbeam, moved forward with a determination that transcended the physical strain. The weight of the wooden burden seemed to mirror the spiritual and emotional weight he carried. As I observed from the periphery, a complex tapestry of emotions unfolded within me. They were getting the best of me as I looked down on the cobblestones in front of me, with drops of his blood smeared by the long robes of the religious leaders in front of me.

The crowd lining the streets bore witness to this haunting journey, their eyes a mixture of curiosity, grief, and, in some cases, defiance. The agony etched on Jesus' face as he stumbled under the load resonated with a profound humanity that transcended the grandeur of the moment.

My duty compelled me to maintain order, yet a profound sense of unease lingered. The trudging steps, the oppressive heat, and the mounting tension created an atmosphere that seemed to suspend time itself. I couldn't escape the awareness that I played a role in this unfolding drama, a participant in a narrative that extended far beyond the temporal realities of the day.

As the journey continued, I found myself wrestling with the gravity of the scene. Golgotha loomed in the distance, a stark reminder of the impending climax. Each step brought us closer to the site of crucifixion, a place where the convergence of divine purpose and human suffering would unfold.

In the midst of this haunting procession, I couldn't escape the feeling that I was not merely a detached observer. The weight of responsibility bore down on me, and the echoes of the crowd's murmurs blended with the haunting sound of Jesus' footsteps. The path to Golgotha became a corridor of introspection, where duty collided with a profound sense of introspection, leaving me to grapple with the unfolding tragedy and the complex emotions that accompanied it.

The scene unfolded before me, surreal and haunting. The cross lay on the ground, a stark symbol of impending doom. As a centurion, I stood stoically, my gaze fixed on the wooden structure that would soon become an instrument of execution.

The soldiers, faces weathered by the harshness of duty, approached the near-lifeless body of Jesus. His limp form, battered and bloodied, bore the marks of the brutal journey to this point. There was a gravity to the air, laden with the weight of the impending crucifixion.

As the soldiers began to drag Jesus onto the cross, I felt a heaviness in my chest. Duty dictated my presence, but a sense of disquiet lingered. The ritualistic preparations for the crucifixion commenced, each movement deliberate and cold.

I thought to myself, could they have planned a revolt just before the crucifixion? It they did, the state of their messiah would certainly draw out the anger in his followers. But if they were to have planned such an event to commence right now, why would Jesus allow his very own mother and aunt and the young disciple he loved the most to be there at ground zero? This doesn't make sense.

And if there were to be a planned revolt, why would we not see crowds armed with spears and knives progressing up this hill of horror?

Bending over the cross, I found myself standing in the midst of a profound moment. I looked into the eyes of Jesus, a gaze that held a depth beyond the physical torment. In that solemn exchange, I spoke for the last time, a question laden with the weight of impending destiny.

"Do you wish to be saved from this fate?" I asked, my voice carrying a muted urgency. His response was a silence that spoke volumes. Jesus, battered and broken, met my gaze with a profound stillness. There was a serenity in his eyes, a resignation to a purpose that transcended the brutality of the moment.

A nod from me signaled the soldier to proceed. The first nail, cold and unyielding, met Jesus' hand. As the sound of the pounding echoed in the air, a collective shudder seemed to ripple through the witnesses. I, too, felt the reverberations of that moment, a collision of duty, destiny, and the profound silence that enveloped the crucifixion scene.

The crucible of Golgotha held us all captive, entwined in a narrative that unfolded with every nail, every gasp, and every lingering echo of finality. As I stood over the cross, a witness to the culmination of this tragic journey, the gravity of the moment settled into the depths of my being, leaving an indelible imprint on the sands of time.

It Is Done

Standing on Golgotha, time seemed to stretch into an agonizing eternity. The atmosphere was thick with a blend of sorrow, indifference, and an unsettling normalcy that defied the gravity of the scene. Jesus hung on the cross, a solitary figure, and around me unfolded a tableau of emotions and actions that painted a surreal backdrop to this crucible of suffering.

At the foot of the cross, I noticed Jesus' mother, Mary, her eyes reflecting the depth of a mother's anguish. Beside her stood a young disciple, a silhouette of devotion in the face of despair. Their presence added a poignant layer to the unfolding drama, a reminder that, amidst the callous indifference, love and grief persisted.

Some of the soldiers, seemingly detached from the gravity of the event, hung around, engaging in games and banter as if this were just another routine day. Their laughter echoed oddly against the stark backdrop of Golgotha, creating a dissonance that intensified the surreal nature of the crucifixion.

Amidst the soldiers' casual demeanor, there were others who couldn't mask their sorrow. Tears flowed freely from the eyes of those who grasped the significance of the moment. The range of reactions painted a complex tapestry – a convergence of humanity's varied responses to the imminent death of a man hanging on a cross.

His labored breaths were a haunting rhythm, accompanied by the groans of those crucified alongside him. The once defiant crowd had fallen into a hushed reverence, as if the very earth sensed the gravity of the moment. I could feel the oppressive weight of this execution, the culmination of a journey that had begun in the quiet garden.

As the minutes stretched into an eternity, the air seemed to pulse with an energy beyond my comprehension. Jesus spoke, his voice a raspy cry that cut through the stillness. "Father, forgive them, for they know not what they do."

His plea for forgiveness echoed in the chambers of my own guilt-ridden soul. What did I know of forgiveness? The man's gaze met mine, and in that moment, I felt a tremor of understanding, a connection that transcended the brutality of my duty.

Darkness descended upon us as the moon passed in front of the sun, a chilling shroud that draped the scene in an otherworldly gloom. The very earth quivered beneath our feet, as if recoiling from the magnitude of the event. I watched, transfixed, as Jesus and the other two struggled for breath. His parched lips parted, and he uttered words that lingered in the air like an ancient incantation: "I thirst."

A sponge soaked in vinegar was hoisted to his cracked lips, a meager offering in the face of insurmountable suffering. His body convulsed with pain, yet an inexplicable serenity radiated from his eyes. Time itself seemed to pause as the man whispered, "It is finished."

As the man's final moments approached, he cried out with a voice that transcended the boundaries of the earthly realm. "Father, into your hands, I commit my spirit." The words hung in the air, a surrender to a destiny beyond mortal comprehension.

His body went limp on the cross, a tableau of surrender that resonated with finality. The weight of that moment hung in the air, a collective breath held as Golgotha grappled with the impending death of the man who hung suspended between heaven and earth.

Time, suspended in the ordeal of Golgotha, seemed to stand still. The convergence of disparate emotions and actions created a tableau that defied understanding. As I stood witness to this surreal blend of the ordinary and the profound, the crucifixion became a trial that tested the limits of human comprehension and the capacity for compassion in the face of an extraordinary tragedy.

Suddenly, the earth beneath us began to tremble. A seismic force rocked Golgotha, and fear surged through the hearts of both soldiers and onlookers. Thunder rumbled overhead, and bolts of lightning streaked across the darkened sky. Although it was three o'clock in the afternoon, the sky was as dark as midnight. The elements seemed to conspire in a symphony of cosmic unrest, as if the very fabric of reality recoiled in response to the unfolding tragedy.

In the midst of this commotion, a palpable fear swept through the soldiers. The ground shook beneath us, and the once-sturdy crosses swayed ominously. Panic seized the hearts of many, and a collective realization dawned – an unsettling acknowledgment that their actions might have invoked the wrath of the divine.

Soldiers, once stoic in their duties, now succumbed to primal instincts of self protection. Fearful whispers spread like wildfire, and in a chaotic frenzy, some abandoned their posts, fleeing from Golgotha as if seeking refuge from the wrath of angered gods. The crucifixion scene was enveloped in a disarray of chaos and uncertainty.

Yet, amidst the pandemonium, a profound revelation began to dawn on me. The cosmic turmoil mirrored the internal storm within my own soul. The pieces of the puzzle fell into place, and the realization struck me like a lightning bolt – Jesus was no ordinary man. The earth-shattering events unfolding before my eyes were a divine response to the crucifixion of one who, against all expectations, emerged as more than mere mortal.

In the midst of the chaos, I found my voice breaking through the uproar. The words escaped me, a proclamation that resonated with both awe and realization. "Truly, this man was the Son of God!" The admission hung in the air, a confession born out of witnessing the cosmic upheaval that seemed to affirm the divine nature of the one hanging on the cross.

As the storm raged and the soldiers scattered, I stood there, a witness to a revelation that transcended the boundaries of the earthly and the divine. In that moment, Golgotha transformed into a sacred ground where the echoes of thunder and the flickering lightning bore witness to a truth that had unfolded in the crucible of chaos – Jesus, the Son of God, crucified for reasons beyond the understanding of mortal men.

As I stood there on Golgotha, the tumultuous events unfolding around me seemed to fade into a distant murmur. A soldier, under my command, stood by my side as we faced the stark reality of the crucifixion scene. The atmosphere was thick with a mixture of tension and an eerie stillness that seemed to hang over the hill.

I gave the order to break the legs of the three men crucified before us, a brutal act intended to hasten their deaths. The soldier, following my command, moved methodically from one victim to the next. The sound of bones snapping pierced the air, a ghastly symphony of suffering ending quickly.

As the soldier approached the two on either side of Jesus, he executed the order without hesitation. The victims, writhing in pain, succumbed to the finality of their fate. However, when it came to Jesus, a profound hesitation gripped the soldier.

He paused; his gaze fixed on the figure hanging in the middle. "He's already dead," he declared, his voice carrying a note of certainty. A peculiar calmness settled over me as I considered the soldier's words. In that moment, a decision stretched out within me, guided by an intuition that transcended the usual course of duty.

Taking up my spear, I approached Jesus, whose stillness belied the chaos surrounding us. With a single thrust, I pierced his side, aiming for his heart. The act was swift, and as the tip of the spear entered his body, blood and water sprayed over me. The visceral spray seemed to suspend in the air, a silent testimony to the profound act that had transpired.

In the immediate aftermath of that moment, an unusual calmness enveloped me. It was as if a divine peace descended upon Golgotha, and

I found myself reflecting on the words Jesus had spoken. He had foretold of his death for the sins of many, and in that moment, I felt a strange reassurance that my role in this tragedy would not be in vain.

The realization washed over me – forgiveness. The spray of blood and water symbolized a spiritual cleansing, a redemption that extended beyond the intuitive reality of the crucifixion. As I stood there, a witness to the aftermath of a profound act, a sense of peace settled within me. The chaos of Golgotha transformed into a sacred moment of understanding, a moment where forgiveness and redemption transcended the brutality of the cross.

Laid In The Tomb

As I stood there, a Centurion named Longinus, overlooking the hill of Golgotha, I couldn't shake the heavy feeling that hung in the air. The sky seemed to mirror the somberness of the scene below, as if even the heavens mourned the events that had transpired. The lifeless body of Jesus, the man they called the Messiah, hung on the cross, a cruel testament to the brutality of the world.

It was my duty to oversee the crucifixion, to maintain order among the onlookers, and to ensure that the execution was carried out efficiently. But as I gazed upon the lifeless form of Jesus, something within me stirred. His words, the aura of compassion that surrounded him, left an indelible mark on my conscience.

As the sun began to dipped over the horizon, casting long shadows across the hill, a group of figures approached the crucifixion site. Among them were Joseph of Arimathea and Nicodemus, both members of the Sanhedrin, men who had, in secret, followed the teachings of Jesus. They moved with a purpose, a determination that spoke of a plan they had carefully crafted.

I watched as they approached the lifeless body of Jesus, their movements deliberate yet filled with a sense of reverence. The small crowd, which had been a discordance of jeers and lamentations, fell into a hushed silence as the men began their work.

Joseph, a man of wealth and influence, stepped forward with a mixture of sorrow and determination etched on his face. Nicodemus, a man of learning, followed suit, carrying a mixture of myrrh and aloes, a fragrant concoction meant for burial. The gravity of the moment wasn't lost on anyone present, and an air of sacred solemnity enveloped the scene.

In the solemn shadows cast by the Golgotha hill, my gaze shifted momentarily to the base of the cross, where a figure sat in quiet anguish. It was Mary, the mother of Jesus, her eyes swollen with tears that mirrored the collective sorrow of those who bore witness to this tragic scene.

As Joseph of Arimathea and Nicodemus carefully lowered the lifeless body of Jesus, Mary's trembling hands reached out to receive her beloved son. She let out a loud moan, as if the spear I used on her son was now piercing her. The weight of grief etched lines on her face, yet there was a profound dignity in her bearing that spoke of a strength drawn from a source beyond the earthly realm.

With tender reverence, Mary kissed the blood-stained face of Jesus, a gesture that transcended the horror of the crucifixion in the ritual of the face kissed with love. The intimacy of that moment, a mother's lips pressed against the bruised and battered features of her child, held a sacredness that resonated through the stillness of the hill.

I observed from a distance as Mary cradled the body of her son in her arms, rocking him gently as if to soothe the pain that no mother should ever witness in her child. Her whispered words of love and comfort seemed to echo through the silence, a lullaby that spanned the years and connected the agony of the present with the innocence of a baby born in Bethlehem.

The memories of a manger in Bethlehem flooded Mary's mind, an association of the divine vulnerability of a newborn and the brutal finality of a crucified Messiah. In that heartbreaking moment, as Mary's tears mingled with the blood that stained her son's face, the circle of love, life and death seemed to converge, and the profound mystery of existence unfolded beneath the shadow of the cross.

The men worked swiftly yet tenderly, their hands guided by a shared purpose. The linen cloths, the myrrh, and aloes were employed in a ritual of care and respect. As I observed from a distance, a profound sense of witnessing an act of profound significance washed over me.

In that moment, still in the end stage darkness of the eclipse, I noticed the stars emerged overhead. I couldn't help but feel a strange mixture of awe and regret. Awe at the courage displayed by these men in the face of adversity, and regret for my role in the events that had led to this point. The air was thick with an unspoken understanding that what unfolded here went beyond the political conspiracies and power struggles of the day. It was a testament to the enduring power of compassion and the unyielding force of a love that even death could not extinguish.

As the procession wound its way from the crucifixion site to the nearby hill, carrying the lifeless body of Jesus, I followed at a distance, my heart heavy with the weight of what had transpired. Mary and other women lead the procession, pausing frequently to pick up some dusty soil and throw into their hair. The rhythmic footfalls on the rocky path seemed to echo the solemnity of the moment, punctuated only by the soft weeping of those who walked beside me.

We approached a tomb hewn into the rock, its entrance a dark portal into the quiet chamber within. The tomb, a two-room structure, held an air of finality that contrasted sharply with the vibrant life that had once emanated from the body now being borne into its depths.

Joseph of Arimathea and Nicodemus, their faces etched with determination, guided the procession into the tomb's rear chamber. There, they carefully laid the lifeless form of Jesus on a stone slab in the back room. The gravity of the act struck me anew as I observed the scene unfold.

Prior to the wrapping, they meticulously cleaned and anointed the body, adhering to the sacred rituals that governed such burials. The scent of the fragrant oils and myrrh lingered in the air, a poignant reminder of the reverence with which this task was undertaken. I couldn't help but feel a strange mix of awe and sorrow as I watched the meticulous care with which they prepared the body of one I strangely now believe is the Messiah for his final resting place.

First, they wrapped the body lengthwise along the back and over the front with linen, each fold a testament to the love and respect they held for the one they considered their savior. A separate head cloth they called the sudarium, enveloped his face, a shroud of dignity in the midst of the profound tragedy.

In the back room of the tomb, sticks of burning incense were placed, their aromatic streams of smoke weaving through the air, a symbol of purification and sanctification. The flickering flames cast dancing shadows on the walls, creating an unearthly atmosphere within the confines of the rock-hewn chamber.

A large round stone, unyielding in its weight, was rolled across the entrance, sealing the tomb with an ominous finality. As the stone settled into place, a heavy silence descended upon the hill, a silence that seemed to reverberate with the magnitude of what had transpired. Men with buckets were there to whitewash the round stone.

We all left the area, the weight of the moment lingering in the air as the tomb stood as a silent witness to the end of a life that had touched the hearts of many. The evening enveloped Golgotha, shrouding the sacred space in darkness, and as we departed, the echoes of a profound chapter in history resonated through the quiet hills.

A Strange Place For A Centurian

The morning sun cast an eerie light on the aftermath of the earthquake that had shaken Jerusalem the day before. As I approached the temple, the once grand and imposing structure now stood marred and broken. The very foundation, a symbol of strength and permanence, had been severed by at least a foot, a gaping wound in the heart of the sacred edifice.

Caiaphas, the high priest, and his father were there, their faces etched with a mixture of anger and despair. They paced before the fractured temple, shouting revengeful words that echoed through the desolate courtyard. The blame fell heavily on Jesus and his followers, as if their mere presence had summoned the wrath of the heavens upon the holy sanctuary.

As I observed the scene, I couldn't help but recall words someone had shared with me, a cryptic statement attributed to Jesus. He had spoken of the temple being destroyed and rebuilt in three days. In the wake of this devastation, it seemed that the fulfillment of those words was being laid at the feet of Jesus' followers.

The once majestic Holy of Holies now stood exposed, its sacred confines laid bare for all to see. The heavy blue, purple, crimson, white and gold colored curtain that had veiled this holiest of places had been torn nearly in two, with only a small section at the bottom still clinging desperately to the frame. It was as if the very fabric of the divine had been ripped into pieces, leaving the leaders of the temple in a state of profound uncertainty.

The wooden ark, gilded inside and outside, had fallen on one side, resting on the handles. The pure gold cover with it's "mercy seat" for the Divine Presence was cocked, clearly exposing the Tablets of the Covenant, and a jar supposedly containing mana from their journey from Egypt. I also saw from my vantage point a table they call the "Table of Showbread", but no bread loaves were visible.

A golden lampstand with remnants of seven broken oil lamps was laying on the floor with a sooty flame oscillated in a rhythmic movement, swaying as it sought oxygen across the floor where the oil had spilled. The only thing I noticed undisturbed was a sacrificial altar made of bronzed boards. I wondered if this little sacrificial table was spared damage intentionally by the Divine.

Caiaphas and his father, in their frenzied deliberations, grappled with the dilemma of what to do with the exposed Holy of Holies and the damage to what was inside. The weight of tradition and sacred protocol pressed upon them, but the earthquake had shattered not only the physical structure but also the spiritual certainties that had anchored their faith.

The task of rebuilding the temple loomed large, a monumental effort that would require years of labor and resources. The temple, once a symbol of enduring strength, now lay in ruins, a tangible testament to the fragility of human endeavors in the face of cosmic forces.

As I stood amidst the wreckage, a witness to the tumultuous aftermath, the words of Jesus rebuilding the temple in three days lingered in my thoughts, leaving me to ponder the enigmatic connection between his prophecies and the unfolding tragedy that had befallen the very heart of Jerusalem. The air was thick with uncertainty, and the once sacred precincts echoed with the tumultuous clash of earthly tumult and divine mystery.

Leaving the shattered remains of the temple behind, I made my way through the distressed streets of Jerusalem. The city, once bustling with life, now wore an air of mourning, mirroring the desolation of the temple. As I walked, reports from people coming in from the countryside reached my ears, each tale more unsettling than the last.

Whispers of the earth itself convulsing with grief and anger spread like wildfire. In the towns and villages surrounding Jerusalem, the very ground had opened up, a bizarre and unnatural occurrence that left the people in stunned disbelief. Strangely, the reports spoke of this phenomenon taking place mainly in the cemeteries where the dead "rested with their ancestors."

It was an unsettling twist to an already catastrophic event. The earth, usually a symbol of stability and continuity, had become a vessel of upheaval, a testament to the power of the divine. The connection between the disturbances in the burial grounds and the destruction of the temple sent shivers down the spine of those who heard the tales.

I couldn't shake the feeling that something profound was still unfolding, something beyond the realm of mere natural disaster. The seismic events seemed almost symbolic, as if the very fabric of life and death had been ripped apart in tandem with the tearing of the temple curtain. Questions and speculations filled my mind, and an undercurrent of fear gripped the hearts of those who witnessed the aftermath.

As I continued through the city, the magnitude of the unfolding calamity became more apparent. The interconnected threads of the temple's ruin and the strange happenings in the surrounding areas wove a tapestry of cosmic disturbance. It was as if the earth itself, in response to the events surrounding the crucifixion and the destruction of the temple, was expressing its turmoil in ways both mystifying and terrifying.

The city's once vibrant streets were now hushed, the atmosphere heavy with uncertainty and foreboding. I couldn't help but wonder if there was a deeper meaning to these upheavals, a cosmic reckoning that transcended the boundaries of mortal comprehension. The reports of the earth's strange convulsions in the cemeteries only added to the mystique, leaving me with a sense that the aftermath of these tumultuous days held secrets that surpassed the grasp of human understanding.

As I walked through the quiet streets of Jerusalem, my mind burdened with the recent events that had shaken the very foundation of the city. The air was thick with an unsettling stillness, and as I approached the house of Joseph of Arimathea, I couldn't shake the feeling that the choices made within these walls of his might shape the uncertain future.

Upon arriving at Joseph's residence, I ascended the steps leading to the back entrance, each footfall echoing with a weight that mirrored the heaviness in my heart. The house, nestled in the shadows of recent upheaval, seemed a refuge of calm amid the storm.

As I reached the top of the steps, I hesitated before knocking on the closed door. The murmurs of conversation from within reached my ears, and I couldn't help but wonder what allegiance Joseph had chosen in the wake of Jesus' crucifixion. My hand rapped gently on the door, a tentative signal of my presence.

A face appeared in the window, peering out with a mix of curiosity and caution. I spoke through the door, my voice carrying the sincerity of my intent. "I come in peace and mean no harm. I just want to talk." The door reluctantly creaked open, revealing a glimpse of those gathered inside.

As I stepped over the threshold, Joseph greeted me with a reserved warmth. He informed me that they were in a period of mourning, engaged in a repast ritual of drinking wine and eating the bread of sorrow. In this upper room, I was introduced to each of Jesus' followers, including his mother Mary, his aunt Mary, and her husband Cleopas. The atmosphere was somber, yet there was an underlying sense of unity among them. His disciples displayed an apprehensive fear, as if they didn't know if they would be next to be arrested and killed.

They sat around a table, each with a partial glass of wine and a plate of bread crumbs in front of them. The symbols of their mourning were laid out, and the room was hushed with a profound reverence. I extended my sincere condolences for the loss of their beloved family member and friend, acknowledging my limited knowledge of Jesus and the Jewish faith.

In response, they invited me to sit among them. The air, heavy with grief, seemed to lighten a fraction as they began to share their memories and love for Jesus. It became apparent that they were not only mourning the loss of a charismatic leader but also facing the daunting uncertainty of a future marked by the ire of Jewish leaders.

Despite my role as a Roman centurion, a representative of the occupying force, they welcomed me into their intimate circle. It was a testament to the depth of their fear and the strength of their commitment to preserving the memory of Jesus and his teachings in the face of potential persecution. As I listened to their stories, a complex tapestry of emotions unfolded within me, revealing the intricacies of a moment in history where lines between allegiances were blurred, and humanity sought solace in shared grief.

As I settled into a seat among them, a respectful hush fell over the room. The flickering candlelight cast shadows on faces marked by grief, yet each eye held a spark, a testament to the resilience within. Joseph, with a solemn nod, gestured for someone to speak.

An elderly man, his weathered hands trembling slightly, began to share his memories of Jesus. His voice held a mixture of reverence and sorrow as he spoke of the miracles witnessed, the parables heard, and the profound impact Jesus had on the lives of those who followed him. It was a narrative woven with the threads of personal encounters, each tale contributing to the portrait of a man whose teachings transcended the ordinary.

Jesus' mother, Mary, spoke next, her words measured but filled with a mother's pride as well as anguish. She recounted moments from his childhood, the tender scenes of a young boy growing up in Nazareth. Her eyes reflected the pain of a mother who had witnessed her son's journey from innocence to a destiny entwined with the divine.

Aunt Mary and Cleopas, his uncle, shared stories of family gatherings, moments of laughter, and the unspoken understanding that there was something extraordinary about their nephew. Cleopas recounted how the whole family was on their way back to Nazareth after a Passover roughly 20 years earlier and discovered that they lost Jesus. He was a youth but was wise beyond his age. He often would be listening as well as sharing the scriptures he learned from his mom in the years he was too young to work with his hands in his father's workshop. His mother and father had to return all the way back to Jerusalem, only to find him fully engaged in conversations with the church elders. He probably had no idea that 20 years later the same group would be trying to put him to death! The room seemed to hold its breath as he described the transformative power of that encounter, a spark of hope in the midst of profound loss.

Others chimed in, sharing anecdotes that painted a vivid picture of the man they had come to love and respect. A woman spoke of the healing touch that had cured her affliction, a former tax collector recounted the day Jesus called him to follow, and a fisherman reminisced about the miraculous catch of fish that had forever altered the course of his life.

The stories flowed like a river, weaving together a cloth of a life that had touched so many which now I can only think of the one which covers his lifeless body. Despite the sorrow that hung in the air, there was an undeniable warmth in the room, a shared camaraderie born out of a common bond and a determination to honor Jesus' legacy. I felt so blessed to be so warmly invited into this circle.

As I listened to their tales, I felt a strange mixture of detachment and connection. These were people, not just followers of a charismatic leader, but they were trying their hardest to emulate the man they loved so much. Their stories painted a complex portrait of a movement that had grown far beyond the expectations of many. The air hummed with a collective determination to keep the flame of Jesus' teachings alive, even in the face of potential persecution.

In that upper room, surrounded by those who had chosen to stay true to Jesus' memory, I found myself at the intersection of duty and humanity. The stories they shared were not only a testament to their grief but also a plea for understanding in a world marked by division. As I absorbed the richness of their narratives, I couldn't help but wonder how these moments would shape the course of history and whether the echoes of their stories would resonate through the ages.

As the evening wore on and the tales of Jesus' life unfolded, a subtle shift in the atmosphere enveloped the room. It was as though an unspoken acknowledgment of the enigmatic events that had transpired during the crucifixion lingered in the air. With a sense of trepidation, I felt compelled to share my own encounter with Jesus.

With a deep breath, I began recounting the events that unfolded in the aftermath of Jesus' scourging. The haunting memories played out in my mind like a vivid tapestry of agony and perplexity. The weight of the flogging, the twisted crown of thorns, and the echoing cries of the crowd seemed to echo in the recesses of my consciousness.

I described the moment when Jesus, bloodied and battered, locked eyes with me. There was an inexplicable connection, an intensity in his gaze that defied the brutality of the scene. He had said to me that his mission is to take on the sin of the world. All sin ever committed and ever to be committed! His mission was to conquer sin through his death and conquer death by rising again! All the time speaking with a gaze that seemed to pierce through the layers of my Roman armor, reaching into the depths of my very soul.

Later, while on the cross, he spoke not with anger or defiance, but with a serenity that confounded my expectations. His words, "Father, forgive them, for they know not what they do," echoed in my mind. In that moment, a profound realization dawned upon me – the man before me was not merely a victim of circumstance but a figure of transcendent grace that I did not understand.

As I shared this encounter, the room fell silent, the weight of the revelation settling upon us. I explained my struggle to comprehend the meaning behind his words. How could a man, subjected to such brutality and injustice, find the strength to utter words of forgiveness? And why did he choose to take on the sins of the world? Questions that had lingered in my mind, an enigma that defied the parameters of my Roman worldview.

Joseph's gaze met mine, his expression a mix of empathy and understanding. The others, too, listened attentively, their eyes reflecting a spectrum of emotions – disbelief, curiosity, and perhaps a glimmer of hope that Jesus' message of love, hope and forgiveness had reached even the man responsible for carrying out the judgment of the governor.

In the midst of that sacred space, a dialogue unfolded. They shared their interpretations of Jesus' teachings, offering insights into the profound wisdom embedded in his words. His call for forgiveness, even in the face of unimaginable suffering, resonated with their understanding of a divine love that transcended human comprehension.

I felt myself being drawn to join them as we grappled with the paradox of a crucified yet forgiving Messiah, the boundaries between occupier and occupied, Roman and Jesus follower, began to blur. In that room, we were not defined by our roles but by our shared humanity and the shared struggle to make sense of a world that often seemed to defy understanding.

The afternoon wore on, and the repast continued, now infused with a deeper layer of contemplation. The wine and bread, symbols of mourning, took on new significance as we collectively wrestled with the profound implications of Jesus' life and death.

As I left the upper room, the weight of the encounter lingered within me. The lines between duty and understanding had blurred, and I found myself standing at the crossroads of a spiritual awakening. The stories shared, the encounters remembered, and the words of forgiveness echoed in my thoughts, leaving me to grapple with the complexities of a truth that transcended the boundaries of the known world.

Pilate's Problem Almost Gone

As I made my way back through the streets of Jerusalem in the afternoon sun, the echoes of the late morning's discussions reverberated within me. The upper room, with its stories of Jesus and the shared contemplation, seemed a world away from the harsh realities awaiting me at Pilate's Palace. My mind buzzed with the complexities of duty and newfound understanding.

Arriving at the palace, I was ushered into the presence of Pontius Pilate. His expression, usually stoic and composed, revealed a flicker of apprehension as he awaited my report. The room, adorned with opulence, seemed to amplify the gravity of the situation.

With measured words, I conveyed my assessment of the current state of affairs in Jerusalem. The city, still reeling from the seismic events of the crucifixion, was enveloped in an uneasy quiet. The followers of Jesus, far from organizing an uprising, were gripped by grief and fear. The Jewish leaders, preoccupied with the aftermath in the temple, showed no signs of orchestrating immediate retaliation.

I could see a glimmer of relief in Pilate's eyes, a confirmation that the immediate threat of an uprising had diminished. Yet, as the conversation unfolded, a new concern emerged – the potential for mischief surrounding the tomb of Jesus. Caiaphas, perhaps fueled by his own fears or a calculated maneuver, had projected onto Pilate the idea that someone might attempt to steal the body and claim a resurrection.

Pilate, caught in the web of political intrigue and the enigmatic circumstances surrounding Jesus' death, sought a solution. He proposed that the tomb be sealed and guarded to prevent any tampering or theft.

The irony of the situation was not lost on me – a Roman centurion assigned to ensure the security of a tomb claimed to house a crucified Messiah.

Recognizing the gravity of Pilate's concerns and driven by a sense of duty, I agreed to lead a detail of soldiers to the tomb of Jesus. The late afternoon air was cooling as we made our way to Golgotha, the place where life had been extinguished just hours before. The flickering torchlight illuminated the rocky path, casting eerie shadows on the rugged terrain.

Upon reaching the still closed tomb, I oversaw the meticulous process of sealing it with metal wires firmly attached to the stone cliff and crossed over the large round stone and affixing the imperial seal of the governor in wax to ensure its integrity. The soldiers stationed themselves around the tomb, ready to thwart any attempts to disturb the supposed final resting place of Jesus. I lit a large fire in front of the tomb not only for warmth thru the cool night I expected, but also to provide light to securely observe all areas around the tomb.

As the night wore on, I couldn't help but reflect on the surreal nature of the task at hand. Here I was, a Roman centurion, guarding the tomb of a man whose followers believed would rise again. The lines between duty and the inexplicable blurred in the silent hours of that night, and I found myself a reluctant guardian of a tomb that held the echoes of a transformative chapter in history. But, what would I do if some of his followers did show up? Would my tender and young faith be shattered? Would there be a confrontation?

The night hung heavy with an uneasy stillness as I stood guard with a detail of soldiers around the sealed tomb. The flickering torchlight and the warming fire cast long shadows on the rocky ground and against the stone face of the hill in front of us, and the air was thick with an eerie tension. The irony of the situation was not lost on me — a Roman centurion, clad in armor and armed with a sword, tasked with guarding the resting place of a man whose life had ended by that very blade.

The memories of the crucifixion replayed in my mind, the gruesome details etched in my memory. I had thrust my sword deep into his chest, the blade piercing through flesh, between ribs until it met the soft resistance of his heart. The vivid recollection of that moment sent a shiver down my spine, and I couldn't escape the haunting image of the fluids in his chest drenching me, a visceral reminder of the brutality of my duty that day.

Now, as I stood sentinel over the tomb, the sealed entrance loomed before me. Earlier in the evening, we had secured the round stone covering with wire, a makeshift but effective deterrent against any unauthorized access. The crossed wires were then covered with wax, and the seal of the governor, unmistakable in its imperial authority, was pressed into the wax.

The precautionary measures were thorough, a reflection of Pilate's concern that someone might attempt to tamper with the tomb. The wax seal, prominently displaying the governor's insignia, served as a visible deterrent and a marker of the grave consequences awaiting anyone who dared to breach the sanctity of the burial chamber.

As the night unfolded, the hushed conversations among the soldiers betrayed an undercurrent of skepticism. Some scoffed at the idea that followers of a crucified criminal would attempt to steal the body, while others traded rumors of the miracles attributed to this Jesus. I found myself caught in the crossfire of skepticism and intrigue, a bystander in a narrative that defied the norms of my Roman worldview.

The hours passed slowly, the night stretching into an endless expanse of uncertainty. I glanced at the sealed tomb, half-expecting the stone to shift or the wax to show signs of tampering. The occasional gusts of wind stirred the surrounding silence, and every creak or rustle heightened the soldiers' vigilance.

As the first light of dawn painted the horizon, a collective sigh of relief swept through the weary ranks. The tomb remained undisturbed, the seal intact. The morning sun bathed the rocky landscape in hues of gold and amber, signaling the end of a night that had held the weight of an unprecedented chapter in my military service.

I couldn't help but wonder about the unfolding events and the mysterious circumstances that had led me from the crucifixion to this silent vigil. The answers eluded me, and as the soldiers dispersed, leaving the sealed tomb behind, I carried with me the residue of a night that blurred the lines between duty, the inexplicable, and the ever-elusive truth.

They Know Not What They Do

The night had lingered long, the air heavy with anticipation as we stood guard over the sealed tomb of Jesus. The flickering torchlight cast dancing shadows on the rocky terrain, and a silence enveloped us, punctuated only by the rustling wind and the distant murmurings of the city awakening.

As the first light of dawn began to touch the eastern sky, a sudden seismic tremor shook the earth beneath our feet. The unexpected quake reverberated through the stillness, and I felt an uneasy disquiet settle over the guarded tomb. The men exchanged startled glances, their stoic composure momentarily shattered.

In the quiet aftermath of the tremor, an unsettling sound echoed through the pre-dawn air. The wire banding containing the round stone, securing the entrance of the tomb, began to pop one at a time. The tension in the wires exceeded its tensile strength, and we watched in disbelief as the stone, heavy and unyielding, started to roll slowly to one side, apparently on its own!

A collective breath caught in our throats as the tomb's opening revealed itself, and an inexplicable brilliance emanated from within. The darkness gave way to an intense light, as if a power beyond mortal comprehension had ignited the very heart of the sepulcher.

In the luminescence, I saw the linen that had shrouded the body of Jesus began to deflate, its form receding as though it had held not a lifeless body, but rather something ephemeral, weightless. The sudarium, covering his head, lay folded neatly on a post in the first room of the tomb, a curious display of divine order amid the unfolding mystery.

The unearthly radiance within the tomb was abruptly replaced by the warm glow of the morning sun cresting the hill. The transition from celestial brilliance to earthly light was seamless, leaving us to grapple with the otherworldly spectacle we had just witnessed.

I stood before the tomb, my breath held in the cold grip of anticipation. The air was thick with the remnants of mourning, and I hesitated, unsure of what awaited within. The entrance loomed like a gateway between worlds, a boundary between the known and the inexplicable.

With a deep breath, I stepped forward, leaning against the stone away to view the sepulcher closely. What met my gaze seized the air from my lungs. The linens that had once enshrouded the lifeless form of Jesus had indeed, now lay crumpled, deflated, as if the very breath of death had been snuffed out.

A shiver ran down my spine, and I blinked in disbelief. The empty linens seemed to mock the laws of nature, defying the logic I clung to as a Roman centurion. My gaze lingered on the vacant cocoon, and a thunderous heartbeat echoed in my ears.

As I turned, expecting solitude, my eyes collided with a figure standing before me. The shock coursed through every power of my being. It was Him – Jesus, not lifeless, but vibrant, radiant, with an unearthly light that banished the shadows from the cavern.

I stumbled backward, my hand instinctively reaching for the hilt of my sword, but my fingers found only emptiness. The weight of my armor suddenly felt burdensome, and I fell to my knees, paralyzed by a force I could neither comprehend nor resist.

"Peace be with you, Longinus," his voice, a melodic resonance that transcended mortal sound, filled the air. "Fear not, for I have conquered death."

The words reverberated through the cavern of my soul, unlocking chambers of understanding I never knew existed. I felt a surge of humility and awe, a recognition of a power beyond the might of Rome.

"Lord," I stammered, my voice strained with emotion, "I am but a humble servant, a centurion at the gate of eternity. I stand before you, not as a conqueror of nations, but as one who beholds the conqueror of death."

With profound reverence, I found myself uttering words that seemed to flow from a source beyond my own understanding. The presence of the Risen Lord before me, coupled with the weight of my guilt for the role I played in His crucifixion, invoked a sacred response. As I knelt, words echoed in my mind, carrying the essence of contrition and acknowledgment of a higher power.

"Oh Lord," I began, my voice resonating with an unexpected clarity, "we have erred and transgressed, our actions casting shadows upon the light of Your righteousness. To You, the sovereign, belong mercy and forgiveness, yet we, in our folly, have turned away and stumbled in the darkness of our deeds."

The words unfolded like a prayer, a plea for mercy and redemption, as the divine presence enveloped the cavern. "We are but dust, and to dust, we shall return. In Your infinite grace, blot out our iniquities, and let the radiance of Your mercy shine upon us."

In that sacred moment, I, Longinus, Roman centurion, offered a humble prayer that seemed to bridge the gap between mortal inadequacy and the divine mercy embodied by the Risen Lord before me.

As the extraordinary events unfolded, the voices of approaching women followers of Jesus reached our ears. Panic seized my detail, and one by one, they scattered, fleeing the scene as if pursued by unseen forces. Left alone, I bent over to pick up some of the broken wire, its crossed ends still intact with the wax seal of the governor.

The approaching footsteps drew nearer, and in that moment, I felt a strange mixture of awe and trepidation. The broken wire in my hand seemed inconsequential in the face of the inexplicable events that had transpired. I made a swift decision to leave the scene and report the unfolding miracle to Pilate.

The air crackled with an otherworldly energy as I left the site, carrying with me the fragments of wire, the wax seal, and the weighty realization that the night had birthed a moment that transcended the boundaries of the known world. The enigma of the empty tomb lingered in the morning air, and as I made my way back to Pilate's Palace, I grappled with the task of conveying the unexplainable to a man whose worldview was anchored in the tangible and the rational.

Entering Pilate's presence, I carried with me the fragments of the broken wire and the wax seal, tangible remnants of the inexplicable events that had transpired at the sealed tomb. The governor's chambers, adorned with lavishness, seemed to shrink in the face of the weighty revelation I bore.

As I presented the evidence to Pilate, his expression shifted from a stoic facade to one of incredulity and apprehension. The broken wire, still holding the intact wax seal, spoke of a disruption in the carefully orchestrated narrative of power and control. The air in the room seemed charged with an unspoken tension as I began to recount the events at the tomb — the seismic tremor, the rolling stone, the unearthly light, and the inexplicable emptiness within.

Pilate's initial skepticism wavered as he grappled with the implications of what I described. His mind, accustomed to the concrete and the pragmatic, struggled to reconcile the surreal narrative unfolding before him. The broken wire, a fractured link in the chain of imperial authority, lay as a testament to a reality that defied the boundaries of human understanding.

However, as the weight of the situation settled upon him, an unexpected anger simmered beneath the surface. The departure of my detail, their abandonment of their post, had not escaped Pilate's notice. His disappointment morphed into a righteous fury, and he laid the blame squarely on my shoulders.

In a harsh and unwavering tone, Pilate issued a command that sent shockwaves through the room. "Longinus, you are to be killed for the negligence of your men."

The gravity of the pronouncement hung in the air, and the realization that my life was to be forfeited for a failure that I, too, could not comprehend, struck me like a heavy blow. The cold steel of another centurion's sword pressed against my skin, the sharpness of its edge a chilling reminder of the impending doom.

In that harrowing moment, facing the inevitability of my own demise, a strange calm washed over me. The echoes of Jesus' words, uttered in the midst of his own suffering, reverberated in my mind. "Father, forgive them, they know not what they do."

Summoning every ounce of strength within me, I repeated those words aloud, not as a plea for mercy but as a proclamation of understanding. The blade descended, severing the fragile thread of my mortal existence.

As the darkness enveloped me, the paradox of the crucified Savior echoed in the final beats of my heart. In that fleeting moment between life and whatever lay beyond, the mysteries of that fateful night at the tomb and the inexplicable grace of forgiveness became the indelible legacy of a Roman centurion who, in witnessing the extraordinary, found solace in the echoes of mercy.

Don't miss out!

Visit the website below and you can sign up to receive emails whenever John H Brennan publishes a new book. There's no charge and no obligation.

https://books2read.com/r/B-A-KVCX-JYQYC

BOOKS2READ

Connecting independent readers to independent writers.

Also by John H Brennan

Thru The First Disciple's Eyes
Thru the First Disciple's Eyes
Through the Eyes of the Disciple Jesus Loved
Through the Eyes of Cleopas

Standalone
Advice From Above
The Rosary Revealed
Yes, I Knew!
Through The Eyes of Longinus

About the Author

John is a cradle Catholic, the middle child of five, who grew up in upstate New York. Vatican Two saved him from learning Latin the year he trained to be an Altar Server. He attended Catholic School until High School when he transitioned to public school. He received two associates degrees from the local Community College, then started a job in a fortune 500 company as a draftsman. He had met the woman of his dreams and they had the first of their children 9 months after they were married. Six months later, the three headed off to the State University of New York at Buffalo where John studied Mechanical Engineering. By the time John graduated with his BS in Mechanical Engineering, they had their second son and headed back to his hometown to continue his 40 year career and have a third son and finally his daughter. He and his wife now have a son in law, a daughter in law and six beautiful grandchildren. Several events led him to deepen his faith – joining a Catholic Men's Bible Study; attending several Catholic Men's Conferences; attending a Catholic Men's Emmaus Retreat as well as being on several Emmaus Retreat Teams (including giving witness talks); attending daily Mass; Praying the Holy Rosary daily and being an Extraordinary Minister of Holy Communion at Church and Nursing Homes in the area. His engineering job brought him across the USA as well as Mexico, Europe and Asia where he enjoyed creating his own personal Pilgrimages to Holy Sites and sharing the experiences and pictures with family and friends. His retirement ambitions include enjoying his children and grandchildren, continued travel to holy sites around the world and sharing his Catholic faith wherever he can.